Cheshire Cheese

and Camembert

To John
Bon Appétit !

Brent

Honeybee
Books

Published by Honeybee Books
www.honeybeebooks.co.uk

ISBN: 978-1-913675-37-0

Cover Image: A postcard entitled 'Ship Canal - Old Trafford' and dated 1916

Cheshire Cheese
and Camembert

A Novel

Brent Shore

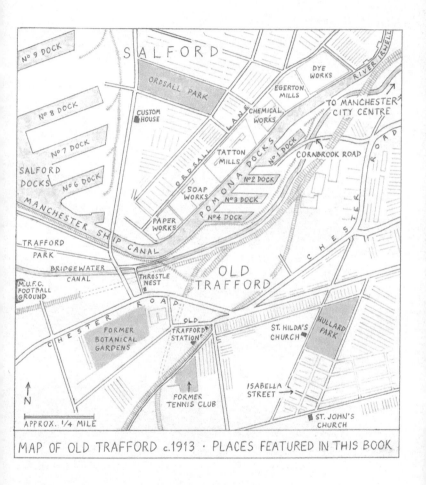

MAP OF OLD TRAFFORD c.1913 · PLACES FEATURED IN THIS BOOK

Contents

See a father with his boy, from single mould be surely cast,
Yet toss it up, that penny piece, its emblem faces to contrast.
Its day and night, its west and east.
Its King and Jack may follow suit but form no perfect pair;
Its saint and sinner, its famine and its feast
Of milk-white Cheshire cheese and yellow Camembert.

lines from *Generations Past*
by Alfred Knott

Prologue
Ralph, like Wolf

✣

How could I possibly have known that everything my mother once told me about my missing father was a pack of lies?

I must have been no more than four years old when she took advantage of a quiet moment – had my sister Mary been sent off on an errand? – to explain, quite abruptly, my father's long and strange absence. An absence so long that I had no real recollection of him beyond an infant's imagination. There was no sound in my memory of a deep, masculine voice in the house, nor smell of a working man's daily sweat, and certainly no vision of a fellow who might look somewhat like a larger version of myself.

"Your daddy died a year ago today," she told me in a soft, measured voice, her dark eyes meeting mine with an intensity that allowed no inch of disbelief. "You know he were workin' up in th'ills, don't you? You remember me tellin' you that, don't you, Charles?"

I must have nodded obediently.

"Listen to me, my lad," she went on. "You're old enough now to be told it all."

I waited, uncertain what to expect, what words I might hear come tumbling from her tongue.

"It seemed there were an accident," she said presently. "A terrible black powder explosion. A shower o' fallin' rocks an' stones."

She gazed at me for a reaction but saw none.

"Your daddy were one o' several navvies who were killed. Caught in t' blast. Caught by rocks, they said. He died fast, they said."

We were sitting together on the dark wood settle that I remember faced the kitchen hearth. Details escape me but we must have still been living in the house in Hyde, not long before we moved up Gee Cross to stay with James. I remember streets, not fields. The light was fading. Or my imagination now presents the room in that way.

With my tiny hands wrapped in hers I listened to my mother's voice, breaking free of her stare for a moment, lowering my eyes to the little silver cross that dangled from a necklace at her throat. The stilted monotone of her delivery was so different from the brisk lightness of her everyday speech. It was like listening to a priest.

"Up in th'ills, miles from here, he were. But I know he died an 'appy man, Charles. He did, I'm sure of it. He loved 'is work, out in th'open in all weathers, part of a gang, a community o' fellas, strikin' out, layin' tracks for t' good o' mankind."

She whispered his name, Ralph; more of a comfort to herself than to include me. There was a catch in her voice; to my ears the word sounded like *wolf.* A tear fell from her cheek.

She was telling me I had no reason to grieve his loss; I could be, should be, proud of him. I let my hands rest in hers, warm and moist, for as long a while as she wanted to hold them. How could I grieve a loss when I never knew him in the first place? You can't lose something you never had, someone you never met.

I said nothing but she saw there was a hint of gratitude in my young eyes. I felt sad because I could sense that my mother was sad, but more than that, I was thankful, I suppose, that she had told me her truth. With my sister sent on her way to run an errand, she had gifted me, and me alone, a most solemn truth.

"We'll speak no more about 'im," she said with a sigh. She released my hands and stroked my cheeks. "It pains me so, Charles. It's been a full year. I have to move along without 'im. Without my Ralph. As do you. But we'll manage, my little man. My strong, brave little man."

I felt a little shiver in my heart as she stood and turned her face away, dabbing her eyes with the cuff of her blouse.

"We'll speak no more about 'im. Not to Mary. Not to another soul."

Stories of tragic accidents on the railways were not so rare in those days as I was growing up. Every year there were sober conversations amongst adults I knew about such incidents. I overheard hushed talk of derailments and the perils of the engineering works. Oftentimes gunpowder was involved: men struck by flying debris, shale and rocks and spinning shards of gritstone – sharp as shrapnel – ripped from the earth; men skidding into ravines that suddenly yawned at their feet; men buried in caves whose roofs split open above their unprotected heads. *Up in th'ills* meant, as far as I could gather, the high Pennines, the wild moors of Lancashire and Yorkshire, the Derbyshire peaks. They were digging cuttings, burrowing tunnels, building embankments and bridges and mighty stone viaducts. Routes were being laid there, I knew, branching away from the established main lines, linking smaller towns and even isolated villages to the expanding network.

And so, my father, this noble Ralph, had been one of the hundreds of victims of the railways, a martyr to modernity and, yes, without bitterness, without regret, I felt a pride in his death. It was over fifty years later, long after my mother had passed on, that I discovered that the story of his demise was a pure fabrication.

Ralph, if such a person ever existed, was not my daddy and never had been. Indeed, if there ever had been a navvy from Hyde called Ralph who toiled up in the hills in the 1860s, who was struck by a torrent of rocks one grim day, his very last as a working man, then he lived and died a very different fellow.

Part One
A Generation Passes

Following the death of Victoria, Queen of the United Kingdom and Empress of India, at the age of eighty-one and after several years of poor health, there was a considerably greater outpouring of national grief than there was for the rather more sudden passing of Martha Rowbotham of Gee Cross, Hyde, Cheshire.

Yet, just two short midwinter days apart, it was clear whose demise was the more shocking. By the January of 1901 Mrs Rowbotham was not yet sixty years of age, and though she had suffered from certain breathing difficulties, they were not considered sufficiently serious to be an imminent threat to her life. Nevertheless, a solicitous doctor gave *pneumonia* as the cause of the poor woman's death and nobody who knew her had reason to dispute his conclusion. For it is a hidden killer, lurking in the diseased creases of the lungs, aggravated in no small measure by year upon year of inhaling cotton dust and particles of smoke. Martha had spent a good portion of her later life as an office worker in the employ of Apethorn Mill, a large, rattling textile factory anchored in the damp valley bottom. However, it seemed that clerical work, practised in well-lit spaces some distance apart from the weaving sheds and the carding rooms, was no guarantee of immunity from the place's insalubrious atmosphere.

I cannot say that I knew Martha Rowbotham well. She was a reticent woman, ill at ease to find herself at the centre of attention, which she rarely was. Grey of hair and always soberly dressed, she nevertheless had a sparkle in her eye to illuminate a bashful smile. She admitted that where she was most at ease was on the arm of her second husband, my friend Walter, invariably together inside the neat little cottage they shared on Jollybant Row, on the main road running down Gee Cross village towards the parsonage and the old Stockport turnpike.

It goes without saying that I met Martha through her marriage to Walter. The very first time he mentioned her to me was the day when, quite out of the blue, he asked me to be the best man at his wedding.

"Who's to be your bride?" I had asked, engaging his broad smile. "Tell me, I need to know."

"It's Martha Harrop," he announced. "You'll recognise her, I'm sure of it. A Gee Cross lady. A widow. She's been looking after my domestics these past twelve months and has been an angel. Really, Charlie, she's the most generous, warm-hearted woman I've ever known."

The pleasure of meeting her shortly afterwards added to the honour I felt at the time in accepting, without hesitation, the fellow's request.

Martha was due some happiness in her life. I have no recollection of John Harrop, her first husband. Neither have I evidence of his treatment of her, honest or otherwise. I do know that many years spent breathing the harmful air of first the spinning rooms and latterly at the carding machines at Apethorn Mill took a deadly toll on the man's health. He was an invalid by his early forties and chronic bronchitis killed him with short delay.

Until taking up with Walter, the woman's consolation was her son Daniel: a kind, sweet-natured lad whom I first met when he was an insecure adolescent. An apprentice fitter at the mill, he earned a modest wage and was protective of his mother, but he lacked anything more than a veneer of confidence in presenting himself to strangers.

"This is our Danny," declared Walter to me during a visit to their home in the days before the wedding.

He was a slight figure, with the round, smooth-skinned face of a child under a mop of unruly brown hair. I offered him a smile and my right hand to shake. Here I was, no more than ten years his senior, a man without airs or graces even if I say it myself. Without a cricket ball in my hand and a flat length of grass to run up on, I would wager I intimidated not a soul.

"Hello, Danny. I'm Charlie. Charlie Knott."

Daniel raised his hand and allowed it to be grasped. For a second he looked at me in the eyes, then down at the floor.

"Pleased to meet you, Mr Knott." It was Walter who uttered the words, observing the formalities in amusement. "Pleased to meet you, Mr Knott. That's what you're to say, Danny. It's polite. I'm sure Mr Knott is pleased to meet you too."

"Pleased to meet you," the boy repeated, before letting his hand fall into the pocket of his breeches. I do not know what Walter had told him about me but the lad could not have been more distressed if he had reported that I had killed a man with my bare fists.

By the time the day of his mother's wedding came around Daniel was a little more relaxed in my company. The happy events of the afternoon provided easy topics for conversation between us and he was genuinely delighted to see his mother at her most contented.

My own wedding was celebrated four years later, by which time I had left Hyde and was living seven or eight miles away in Salford. Most fortuitously, the house in which I rented a pair of rooms belonged to the father of Ada Dooley, a free-spirited and self-confident woman who was to become my wife. Naturally, Walter and his family were invited to the ceremony, but I remember there was a doubt as to whether the old schoolmaster was well enough to travel. It was by no means a simple journey by carriage, train and tramway and, as I recall, autumnal showers made for an inclement period of weather. Nevertheless, the three of them did attend, although I dare say that Danny, by then a more robust twenty-year-old, would have preferred to stay in Hyde and spend the day with friends of his own age. As I said, however, he was devoted to both his mother and his step-father, and if they had asked him to accompany them to Salford, Bradford or even Oxford then he would not have thought twice about agreeing.

They departed early, once our wedding breakfast was over in fact, but it was on Martha's account rather than her husband's. I remember Walter apologising on behalf of his wife, who, in fits of coughs, was being helped into her coat by her son. She was feeling unwell, a little breathless, and wanted to get home to a warm bed as quickly as possible.

Walter Rowbotham was the schoolmaster at the chapel school in Gee Cross for twenty years. Hundreds of boys and girls passed through his care, some less gratefully than others, I suppose, some more eager to quit the academic environment he strove to foster which brought a sense of achievement to some and discomfort to others. Amongst the long list of scholars were both myself and Daniel Harrop, both eternally grateful for the man's contribution to our education and, indeed, to our development. In the face of paternal absence or incapacity, Walter became, by accident and several years apart, a father figure for the both of us. He was a man of integrity and common sense: fussy, he would concede, (actually quite relentlessly pedantic) and with a notion of religious service which I particularly was happier to ignore. Nonetheless his pupils knew that, for all his idiosyncrasies, he had our best interests at heart. He was kind, selfless and, with his favourites, rather indulgent. For those pupils like Daniel and myself he inspired a love of learning and a love for the man himself.

Strangely enough, nobody thought more highly of Walter than a fellow who had no formal education to speak of, a man twenty years his senior: James Shore, my Uncle James, whom I only really knew as a rough-speaking, confused old man. James was not my real uncle but a distant cousin of my mother who offered to share his home on Gibraltar Row with us when she fell on hard times. He kept a sharp eye on my schooling and encouraged me to help him with a basic level of reading. When my patience ran out – I was a flighty young boy, after all – he would trudge all the way up Apethorn Lane, up the Gerrards to the schoolhouse for instruction from Mr Rowbotham himself. During the later years of James' life the pair became most unlikely friends.

As for me, Walter seemed to take on the mantle of uncle after James' passing: he was someone who kept an eye out for me. Like a dependable boiler it was a friendship that remained warm even if left, seemingly neglected, for an age. An arranged meeting or a chance encounter could fire up the flames once again with very little effort. From time to time he might write me a short letter, neatly addressed to my abode in Salford; to my shame I did not regularly respond. I told myself that I had no time, I was absorbed in my working life, in my new family miles away from Hyde. When we spoke our topic was frequently politics, sharing views on the state of our nation. He was always interested in my cricketing exploits, such as they were. And latterly, without fail, he would offer a word or two about the fortunes of Hyde Football Club, his local team. It never failed to amuse me how the bookish old schoolmaster had embraced a sport in which rumbustious young men kicked and chased a heavy leather ball around a muddy field. He saw less and less of the team as his health deteriorated. His eyesight began to fail him and he would complain of the cold even on what felt to me like a mild day. Moreover, a curving spine was imposing a stoop to his gait.

In the years following the loss of Martha, it was generally acknowledged that the joy in Walter's life had largely dimmed, never to reignite. He shared the cottage with Daniel: a strange couple, two men with over forty years between their ages, one time master and pupil, tied together by their devotion to Martha and then, symbiotically, by their reliance on each other. Róisín Quigley, the daughter of the shoemaker, was paid to come in five days a week to cook their meals, wash their clothes and keep the place tidy. There were times when I wanted to shake the old fellow out of his melancholia, out of his inertia, but although he would smile, admit to his self-pity, and promise to make an effort to cheer himself up – with a short walk into Sugarloaf Wood or by reading a chapter or two from a book or spending half an hour at the piano – I knew that his spirit was broken.

One morning in February (the year was 1911), an envelope was passed to me as I was sitting at my office desk. The stamp it bore was franked *Hyde Post Office*. I did not recognise the hand. Inside was a single sheet of crisp white paper upon which, below the address of the parsonage in Gee Cross, three short paragraphs were composed in the same script:

Dear Mr Knott,

I hope you will forgive my taking the liberty of researching your place of work and contacting you without warning in this way. It is many years ago now, but I have not forgotten you playing cricket with us in the Chapel team for a season or two: a fearsome young bowler, as I recall.

I write with regard to the health of a much-respected former colleague of mine, the schoolmaster at Hyde Chapel, Mr Walter Rowbotham. I know that we share an affection for Walter and a concern about his welfare. Indeed, he mentions your name to me very regularly.

Sadly I must inform you that Walter's health has taken a serious turn for the worse in recent days. I have been told that the problem is with his heart. To compound matters, he complains that he is, to all intents and purposes, blind. His stepson Daniel is providing support, of course. All members of our church pray for him – indeed, for the both of them.

With my sincerest sentiments,

Grüss Gott,

Henry E. Dowson

I responded with a letter of my own, thanking the minister

14

for his message and promising that I would visit Gee Cross at the earliest opportunity. Unhappily that opportunity came too late. About a week later, the Reverend Dowson was in contact with me once again, this time by means of the telephone. It was a surprise to hear his voice at the receiver; later I remembered that my letter to him had been sent on business notepaper which had printed upon it the telephone number of our new office exchange.

The moment the old man introduced himself, I knew what he was about to tell me: Walter had passed on before I had the chance to shake his hand, to hear his wise words, to see his faint smile of resignation one final time. He was eighty-one years old.

His funeral was held at the chapel on a bitterly cold morning at the beginning of March. There was as yet no sign of spring and the sky was a high, colourless veil of sorrow. Across the lane from the chapel gates I noticed, with some surprise, the imposing brick and stone building of the new school that had replaced the one where Walter had taught so assiduously. The place was silent, its doors and windows locked tight against the wind. Almost twenty years had passed since I left Hyde and, logically, I should not have been taken by surprise at all. Later on in the same day, I was told that Gerrard's Street had been renamed Stockport Road. I couldn't for the life of me think why. And the Boy & Barrel, a popular alehouse at the top end of that thoroughfare, had disappeared, demolished not long since.

I joined the congregation alone and struggled to find a familiar face amongst the mourners. There were many of Walter's former pupils who had remained in the village but I recognised none of my contemporaries. Mr Dowson led the service and the chief mourners were three men all in their early middle age: Daniel Harrop, of course, and Walter's two nephews who had travelled from the West Riding of Yorkshire with their young families. The brothers were both engaging fellows who introduced themselves to me at the conclusion of the service. Their father and mother, Walter's sister, had both passed away in recent years, and while the elder brother had inherited their farm, the younger was a veterinarian, he told me, specifically a doctor of horses.

A score of us retired to the Cheshire Cheese for refreshments. A fire crackled in the grate and the atmosphere was convivial. I was happy to raise a glass of ale to the memory of my old teacher and friend and, as it happened, spend a little time with Danny. I recall pulling him away from a group of women, who were drinking gin and cackling like a gaggle of geese: former pupils of Mr Rowbotham, clearly boring the man with raucous tales of classroom misdemeanours from the old days.

"Let me buy you another drink, Danny," I said, tugging at his sleeve and leading him away from the ladies, so absorbed in their reminiscences that they barely noticed his extrication.

"Thanks, Mr Knott," he whispered with a grin on his face. It was good to see him smiling, even on a day like this. Especially on a day like this. I remembered the broken tooth he presented to the world whenever he opened his mouth. He had vainly attempted to tidy his hair and he wore a grey suit a size or two too small for him.

"How are you?" he asked. "How's the family? How's the docks?"

"I'm very well, thank you," I replied, offering him a cigarette which he declined with a brisk shake of the head.

And I *was* very well, thank you. I had no regrets about leaving Hyde for work in Manchester. I was happily married to my sweet Ada and the father of our dear son Alfred, who was sixteen at the time, an apprentice newspaper reporter and, to my mind, a most promising cricketer.

"We moved into a larger house a few summers gone," I went on, passing him a glass of ale and leading him over to a corner of the bar. "Closer to th'office. An' it's in a nicer part. Old Trafford. I don't suppose you know it?"

"No. I dunna get down to Manchester that much." He took a sip of his beer. "Well, never, to be honest. Never hardly get out from round here."

I lit my cigarette and took a long drag on it. I gently blew away the smoke and looked him in the eyes.

"Well, happen you should, Danny. You still down at Apethorn Mill?"

"Aye."

"How long's that then? Since you left school, in't it?"

"Aye. Getting' on for twenty-five year."

"You must be a bloody good fitter by now."

He laughed.

"You must have repaired ev'ry bit o' machinery in th'whole bloody mill by now!"

"Feels like it sometimes!"

"Not a nut you've not tightened."

He laughed again.

"Not a cog you've not oiled, eh?"

There was a sudden commotion in the room as a group

began saying farewells and all acknowledged Danny before taking their leave of the establishment.

"So, what's next, Danny?" I asked presently. "Another twenty-five year wi' the same box o' tools?"

He was staring at his glass.

"Dunno."

"Have you thought of a change?"

"Dunno."

"What's there to keep you here now, any road?"

"In Gee Cross?"

"Aye."

He took a long drink from the glass.

"Well, I do like the cottage," he said after a moment.

"There's other cottages, you know."

"An' I 'ave me pals."

"You can make other pals, Danny. An' there's nowt stoppin' you comin' back up here an' seein' your old uns."

"Comin' back up here? Where've you got me livin', Mr Knott? You're workin' on a plan for me, are you?"

I smiled.

"Not really. You make your own decisions. But you could do a lot worse than Manchester, you know. Or even Salford, down on Pomona, on the canal near where I work. There's hundreds o' jobs for mechanics. On the docks, on the ships even. An' there's new factories goin' up every other week. An' I dare say you'd be better paid there than in the mills round here an' all. You could name your price, a proper experienced fitter like yourself."

"I dunno," said Danny, running a hand through his hair for a moment like a schoolboy trying to solve a teacher's puzzle.

"I bet Walter wouldn't expect you to stay in Jollybant Row now that he's gone. Now that him an' your mam are both gone. It was his house. Their house."

"Suppose so."

Having said my piece, by no means something that I had rehearsed, I picked up my glass and drained the last of the beer. There was no reply from Danny. He was scratching his chin, staring at the coals glowing orange in the hearth.

"I thought I might move to Ashton," he said, almost to himself.

I paused, dismissing the idea.

"Manchester's the future, Danny," I asserted. "It is that, an' no mistake. It's leavin' the mill towns behind. Walter would always want the best for you, you know that. An' there's so many opportunities these days. There's a new century started, if you'd not noticed! I've seen it happenin'. Prosperity for everyone, believe you me."

And so Walter's passing was yet one more on the list of those I had known in my younger days, a generation who, quite suddenly, were no longer with us. They were figures who had made an impression on me, some greater than others, understandably, but faces I associated with that time of my own journey from a boy to a youth to a man. They were faces from the dark, old century: Uncle James, born in 1820, my own mother Elizabeth (who died of apoplexy and took her secrets with her to the grave), Martha Harrop, Walter's sister and brother-in-law from Saddleworth, and now the old schoolmaster himself. It struck me that only the formidable Reverend Dowson remained: the indefatigable minister, the Grand Old Man of Hyde (as many called him), who clearly had God batting on his side.

In 1911 I was approaching my fiftieth year. I was in generally good health and thoughts of my own death rarely buffeted my sense of optimism. For, as I had told Daniel Harrop, I was convinced that the new century offered progress in every area of our lives: in politics and education, in medicine and science, in industry and trade. And not only did I believe in a prosperous future, I was lucky enough to be living in the city of Manchester – a modern, regenerating metropolis at the very heart of it all.

Part Two
1913

1

It was generally a walk of fifteen minutes between Isabella Street and the Booth & Byrne offices on Cornbrook Road, whose upper storey windows offered a splendid view of the Number One Dock at Pomona. Punctually leaving the house at a quarter to eight each morning, I would follow the Chester Road north and set my face against the multitude heading south towards Trafford Park.

The road was wide enough for traffic of all kinds: from rattling handcarts to polished Fords pumping petrol fumes into the air behind them. Snorting horses pulled overloaded waggons, motor cars were driven by men (who were rich) wearing goggles, gloves and leather helmets, and electric trams rumbled along, hooked to their overhead cables, filled with factory workers (who were not). Motorised trucks, their engines coughing, their horns honking, were being steered warily between men and women who strode here and there into their path, chattering and chirping, without a thought of danger. There was that fellow on a bicycle I saw now and then: whistling to himself, pedalling up the kerb and on to the pavement to avoid a barrow. Last week he just about stopped himself from running into the back of a lad selling newspapers; no harm done. The pedestrian traffic too was relentless at this time of the morning, as wave upon wave of human energy emerged from the streets of the city: labourers, clerks, technicians, artisans, young and old, some in groups, some alone, some with nails on their boots clicking on the cobblestones. Some wore overalls, some clutched a sack of tools or a cloth bag with their snap inside, others held a well-worn umbrella, just to be on the safe side. Some men wore a cloth cap and a knotted scarf, many of the women and girls would have a shawl wrapped around their shoulders against the cool morning air. Some were jaunty and had a spring in their step, others looked morose, shuffling along reluctantly, a smouldering cigarette stuck to their bottom lip.

A person from a tranquil country parish, a gentle villager more accustomed to the rustic lane, the meandering byway or the little-trod bridlepath, now set down on to these bustling streets, might have been fearful of being swept away by such a deluge, of being overwhelmed by what appeared to be a surging army of men and their machines. All were on their way to a job of work, to earn a living, to share the riches of the vast industrial enterprise that had grown up in less than twenty years at the eastern end of the Manchester Ship Canal.

Meanwhile, wheezing locomotives squealed along the tracks behind the streets: passenger trains with their human cargo, and great engines heaving waggon after waggon of coal or cotton or machinery of some description. The early morning smells were familiar: coal fumes, motor exhausts, engine oil, horse muck and tobacco smoke. And some days, dependent on the direction of the wind, the acrid stench of the dye works which I couldn't abide.

The sprawling new docks were the destination for many of these toiling folk. There were four docks at Pomona, to start with, parallel rectangular basins of water, berths for smaller vessels sailing to and from our closer foreign trading ports. As they clung to the docksides, huddled in their rows, locked on to the dry land for sustenance and supplies, the ships oftentimes reminded me of a litter of piglets suckling at the teats of a mother sow. The larger Salford Docks, a little distance away, included the huge Number Nine Dock which had been ripped out of the land that until ten years ago was a race course for thoroughbred horses. Here sat the larger ships, linking our city with ports far away across the Atlantic Ocean and yet others on the coasts of Africa and India and unimaginably distant Australia. Along the wharves, set back from the railway lines, were warehouses and brick-built storage sheds of all sizes. Nearby there were garages and stables, oil depots and electricity stations and vast coal yards. Rising into the damp, grey sky were the arms of the great cranes: hydraulic cranes, electric cranes, mighty steam-driven cranes.

Spawned by the docks was an explosion of neighbouring industry. Established textile mills now found themselves competing for labour with a soap works, a paper mill, several brickworks, countless engineering works, a great granary and a timber yard – most of which had planted themselves on the wide blade of land bordering the Trafford Wharf, directly opposite the jaws of Salford Docks. New smoke-stacks pointed to the heavens – Mancunian heavens most usually hidden by banks of stubborn clouds drifting eastwards over the simmering city.

For some reason on this June morning I chose to avoid Chester Road and, in spite of the dampness in the air, I took the slightly longer path via Throstle Bank, crossing the railway lines and skirting each of the Pomona Docks in turn. Activity had already begun. Number Four sheltered a tug-boat and a fully-laden Lancashire coal barge; the wharf was empty save for some half-stacked trolleys and coils of rope sitting in puddles of oily water. Number Three was busier, its basin cluttered with small cargo ships, its wharf populated by men in overalls and dotted with crates and barrels and open-backed trucks. Number Two was equally busy, cranes already hauling great crates into gaping holds to the bellowed instructions of the foremen. Meanwhile the grey waters of Number One Dock were occupied by a single larger freighter, a Dutch vessel whose unloading, to shouts and whistles from several labourers, was about to start.

As I knew they would be, the double doors to the Booth & Byrne Company building were already unlocked. The vestibule was warm and brightly lit against the gloom. Through a partition door I could hear the steady chatter of workers readying themselves for the tasks ahead: there on the ground floor about a dozen of them, principally in reception and accounting. I climbed the staircase to the first floor and strode into the wide illuminated space where two of my colleagues, early birds in almost matching suits, were hovering by one of the desks in deep conversation. They looked up simultaneously as I passed them on my way through to my office.

"Good morning, Mr Knott," said Mr Dewsbury; bespectacled, the wearer of a floral bow-tie, the older of the pair.

"Good morning, Mr Knott, sir," echoed Mr South; eager by temperament, his face an open book, the younger man.

"Mornin," I replied. "Mr Dewsbury. Mr South."

That was the extent of it for the moment. Everyone knew what I was like for the first ten minutes of a working day. I needed to settle into my private space, remove my coat and light myself a cigarette.

My office was a good-sized room with a heavy door, upon whose out-facing side was screwed a square brass panel bearing my name and status in capital letters: MR CHARLES KNOTT : OPERATIONS MANAGER. I had a pair of comfortable armchairs for visitors to sit in and a wide window which gave on to a slice of the rectangular basin of Number One Dock. Today it afforded me a raised prospect of the cargo ship *Wolderwijd*. Beyond its faintly steaming funnel, beyond the shifting cranes, I could see the half-mile of opposite shoreline, dominated by a series of bulky brick edifices, each pinned by its soaring chimney: from left to right there stood Tatton Mills, then a chemical works, next along was the Egerton textile mill, and finally the dye works, each one leaking its particular fumes, each one casting a shadow even on a day without sunshine, each one contributing to a familiar Salford skyline.

There was a tap on the door and Mr South appeared.

"Mr Knott, sir," he said, straightening both his tie and his hair as he hesitated on the threshold. "I have your newspaper."

I placed what remained of my cigarette in the ashtray.

"Thank you, Mr South," I said, beckoning him to advance. "Is there any sign of Ethel this mornin', then?"

"We've not seen her as yet, sir, no. She'll not be long, I'm sure. Doesn't she have errands to run for her father some Thursdays, sir?"

I remembered that she had warned me of such an eventuality. Her father was an invalid. She had made a point of asking permission, of course. She was a good woman, not the type that would take advantage.

"Aye, you're right, Mr South," I said, scanning the front page of *The Manchester Guardian*. "If she's not in before ten, have another girl come up. I'll be needin' some dictation takin'."

"Before ten, sir?" South checked his pocket watch. "I'll not forget. Can I fetch you a cup of tea in the meantime, Mr Knott?"

"Aye, you can, Mr South. Thank you. That'd be grand."

I was proud of that brass plaque. Oftentimes I would give it a little polish with my shirt cuff if there was nobody around to bear witness to what I suppose was my vanity.

I had been blessed with a modicum of talent and I had the good sense and resolve to make the most of it. I soon discovered that I could not hope to be successful at every endeavour I put my mind to, but that if I gave the *impression* of competence, then people (employers, colleagues, customers) would find me credible. And that even if a task was beyond my measure, nine times out of ten things would work out perfectly well in any event. Mastery of one's brief was overrated. The *appearance* of mastery was far more important.

A belief in oneself was equally significant: something I had always tried to instil in my son's psychology, although the older he got the less notice he took of any advice from me. As for me, I have had many a dispute with my various employers down the years. I dare say I was at fault on at least half of those occasions, but by force of argument I was able to plant a seed of doubt in the mind of my opponent and so invariably won the day. In a battle of rank it is hard for an underling to triumph; in a battle of confidence, less so.

I had finally left Hyde in 1892. Since my last days as a schoolboy, I had worked as a boilerman's apprentice, a post-office clerk, a bank teller and a pen-pusher at the Town Hall. Arithmetic had been a strength of mine ever since I was an infant making patterns on the floor with the buttons borrowed from my mother's sewing box. Education was my ticket to enter a world beyond the mills and for that I am grateful to my mother and more especially to the quite different contributions of James Shore and Walter Rowbotham. Alerted to the opportunities offered by the Ship Canal project and its impact on the Manchester economy, I moved to the city, quickly securing a secretarial job with one of the companies involved in the construction of the canal and its docks. I found a suitable place to live in a pair of rented rooms in the Ordsall district of Salford.

My landlord was a genial soul, a canny entrepreneur called Mr Dooley, the son of Irish immigrants who by the age of forty owned not only a terrace of back-to-back houses around the corner from St Clement's church, but also a family home and a ladies clothes shop a couple of miles away in Chorlton-cum-Hardy. During the first year of our acquaintance the fellow was happy to chat to me about the process of completing the purchase of a second Dooley's Fashion Store, this one in Cross Street in the centre of Manchester. He also had a beautiful daughter whom I was fortunate enough to meet and fall in love with. Ada and I married in 1893. With considerable parental assistance we bought a home near Salford Infirmary; later we moved to the house on Isabella Street where we live to this day: a short walk to the docks yet close to a park, churches and the fields which border Moss Side. At one time there were botanical gardens and tennis courts nearby but things have changed a little of late. In those early days I felt like living in Old Trafford was being a part of an urban village, if such a thing exists.

By the time the canal opened in 1894 I was working as a book-keeper for the Ship Canal Company itself in an office in the centre of the city. Alfred was born later that year: golden blond as an infant, his hair turning a deeper brown like his mother's as he grew up. Our move coincided with my securing a position as a clerk in the offices of the Port Authority, and through their services I became acquainted with many of the shipping agents who facilitated the expanding trade that the port of Manchester was then accommodating. As the new century dawned, I was offered a job as an accountant with one such shipping agent, the well-established company of Booth & Byrne. I joined them in 1901 and have been steadily and successfully raising my profile there ever since.

And what exactly was it that we did at Booth & Byrne? It was a question that many have asked me, not least Mr Dooley himself. Daniel Harrop posed the same question, one of several curious folk in the Cheshire Cheese after Walter's funeral. In simple terms, we acted as an intermediary, a broker, if you like, between ships looking for cargo to transport and cargo looking for ships to transport it. We offered local expertise to shipping companies to deal with the loading and unloading of freight, associated administration, customs clearance, registration with the Port Authority and so on. From the traders' perspective, we could arrange passage for goods to be exported and facilitate the expediting of imported goods. Well, that was the theory. In any event, and for want of a better explanation, that's more or less what it says on page one in the Booth & Byrne company directory

I have to hand. The one whose latest edition I helped to write.

When the telephone rang I had just begun to read a story in the newspaper about the well-known suffragette activist Emily Davison, who had been seriously injured in a shocking incident during the Epsom Derby.

I unhooked the mouthpiece and, lifting the receiver to my ear, heard an indistinct masculine voice:

"Hello? Hello? Am I speaking to Charlie Knott?"

"Aye. Who's askin'?"

"It's Osmund. Osmund Pollitt."

"Oh, Osmund. Sorry, I didn't recognise your voice."

A white-haired sexagenarian, Osmund Pollitt was the managing director of Booth & Byrne, speaking from his spacious office in central Manchester.

It was true that in those days I hardly recognised anybody's voice at the end of a telephone line, not even my own wife's. Beyond the flattening of tone in the narrow range of audible frequency afforded by the devices, the regular echo and occasional apian hum added to the distraction. The latest models supplied to the company were no improvement; in fact, to my ears, the very opposite. Mr Horridge, the most ancient and irascible member of the accounts team on the ground floor, had no time at all for telephones; he hated the contraptions, preferring to trail up and down stairs to speak to someone in person or, in the case of a communication over a longer distance, he was more likely to send a message scribbled on a postcard. Under duress he would ask one of the juniors to make or receive telephone call on his behalf, to much discreet amusement.

"I've a date for your calendar," said Pollitt briskly. He was not a man to engage in inconsequential chatter if it delayed the work of the day.

"Very good," I responded, extracting a desk diary from beneath a pile of papers I had been studying the previous evening. Opening it in anticipation, I asked:

"What's this then, Osmund, a day out at the cricket? You got a pair o' posh seats for the Worcester match, then?"

Like me, Pollitt was a supporter of Lancashire County Cricket Club, our very local team whose ground was not much more than a mile from my front door. Unlike me, Pollitt was a club member and had access to seats in the private enclosure in the main stand. I could hear him laughing to himself.

"No, it's not a cricketing matter, Charlie. It's business, I'm afraid. We've got a management meeting, hastily arranged, I'm sorry, but that's the way it is now and again."

"For when?"

"Monday the sixteenth. Irish trade and the new regulations coming in from the USA to consider. There'll be a couple of foreign guests. And your presence is required. It'll be all day, I'm certain of it."

"Where? Pomona or up there?"

"Yes, here, of course. HQ. Be here for half past eight. I'll speak to you again beforehand. What you'll need to bring along and so on."

"Indeed."

A dry click signalled the end of the conversation. Pollitt had hung up his mouthpiece; the dialogue was over. He was a funny old soul: light-hearted and whimsical in his esoteric way when he was away from the duties of his office, and yet quite the reverse in his business suit – single-minded, focussed, almost dour. I retained a soft spot for the man; after all, he had given me my job with the company and had promoted me as swiftly as was appropriate. I knew his family superficially: a strait-laced wife and two plain daughters, twins in their thirties, neither married.

In the company hierarchy Pollitt was one rung below greatness. The chairman, Mr Byrne, whose Christian name of Martyn I was never encouraged to employ, was quietly spoken, had grown rather stout in his later years and maintained a reputation as a most shrewd businessman. He owned fifty-five per cent of the company, so it was said, increasing his share upon the untimely death of his long-time partner Mr Booth, who, while alive, was an engaging if somewhat arrogant fellow: the usage of his forename Jonathan also not encouraged among underlings. Mr Booth's son, also Mr Booth (christened Jacob), had been persuaded to sell a portion of the family shares, partly to cover death duties and to pay to take his bereaved mother on an extravagant Mediterranean cruise. Once returned to England, he was a minor contributor (according to rumour) to a restructuring of the company; it was a process which resulted in his dispatch to the port of Liverpool, where he was to oversee Booth & Byrne's operations at the western end of the canal. As such, "young" Jacob was little seen in Manchester these past two years.

Ethel had appeared in the meantime. I heard her raspy voice in the main office well before she knocked, pushed open the door and peered into mine. She complimented me on my choice of necktie, as she did from time to time. She removed my empty teacup and five minutes later returned bearing a fresh one.

I picked up the newspaper. Emily Davison had made quite a name for herself, and indeed for her cause. As the Derby reached its final stages, as the stampede approached Tattenham Corner, so ran the report, she had dashed out from the crowd of spectators, breaching the fence and into the path of the onrushing horses, waving a suffragette flag. It seems that she had targeted the King's own horse, the colt Anmer, causing it to fall, bringing down the unsuspecting rider and inevitably causing untold injuries to herself in the process. Anmer was the least affected by the incident: he finished the race riderless. Herbert Jones, the unfortunate rider selected to wear the King's colours, was concussed and suffered broken ribs. Miss Davison, a veteran of the struggle for female enfranchisement who had spent many a stretch in prison for her troubles, now lay unconscious in a London hospital bed.

I swallowed a mouthful of Ethel's sweet tea and put away the newspaper.

I knew someone who would be upset and yet in all likelihood inspired by the gesture. My wife Ada was a supporter of the suffragists and a regular attendee at meetings. She was less enthused by the suffragettes and their disruptive actions but nonetheless admitted to admiring the likes of Miss Davison, and above all, Emmeline Pankhurst, our Mancunian firebrand. It was out of the question that Mrs Pankhurst would have a public comment on the events at Epsom, however, she herself, as far as I recalled, being currently detained at His Majesty's pleasure.

It would be reported four days later that Miss Davison had died in hospital from a fracture to the base of her skull.

2

The day's rain had stopped but the air was still cool for early summer. I decided to walk home by the docks. Tugboats and other smaller craft were patrolling the dark waters of the basin. On the wharf of Number Two Dock, cranes were still heaving strapped-up crates into the hold of this ship or lifting cargo from the bowels of that one. I was wary of locomotives lumbering close to where I trod. Labourers with handcarts weaved between stacks of great wooden boxes, avoiding the puddles. Some men led horses pulling cumbersome waggons, some stood giving orders between cigarettes, bellowing instructions up to the deckhands. One or two recognised me and waved a gloved hand in my direction.

These sights were as familiar to me as my own parlour, yet there were times when I stepped back to marvel at what had been achieved here these past twenty years. It was no exaggeration to call it a miracle of civil engineering. From an industrial hub almost totally reliant on the port of Liverpool for its imports and exports, Manchester now controlled its own inland port, forty miles from the open sea yet extensive enough to serve the largest of ocean-going vessels. Naturally there had been great opposition to the Ship Canal, not only from the railways and the authorities in Liverpool (wary of losing income from shipping and storage fees) but also from Parliament itself – for reasons I could never understand. I do consider myself to be an intelligent man and yet it was not unusual for me to fail to comprehend the rationale of our elected representatives.

Nevertheless, here I stood, at the heart of commercial activity that could hardly have been imagined a generation ago.

Liverpool had no choice but to give up a share of its trade: wheat imports, oil and livestock were still largely controlled there whilst Manchester had grown prominent in the importation of raw cotton, timber, grain, tea and tropical fruits. Meanwhile coal, salt, textiles and machinery were amongst our most significant exports. I guessed that such commodities were being charged on to ships before my eyes at that very moment.

Five minutes later I turned the corner to cross the bridge by Throstle Nest and found myself following a fellow that I fancied I knew, not only by his gait but also by his thatch of greying hair. He was carrying a cloth bag which appeared weighed down by hand tools. It was past six o'clock and the pathway was busy with pedestrians homeward bound. Not everybody was heading in the same direction, however, and as a pair of young women strolled gaily towards us, arm in arm, engrossed in their lively conversation, the man stopped in his tracks and turned to watch their sprightly passage. I saw immediately that it was Daniel Harrop. He could not fail to notice me as I caught him up.

"Danny!" I called.

"Mr Knott? Is that you?"

"Who else could it be?" I said, smiling and patting him on the sleeve. "You eyein' up those two lasses, then?"

The women were already out of sight, swallowed up in the steady flow of folk behind us. Danny laughed, self-consciously, revealing his broken tooth.

"Aye, well, they were a sight, weren't they? I wonder where they were off?"

"You want to go after 'em an' ask?"

"Better not."

"Oh aye?"

"A married man these days, Mr Knott."

"Are you? I'd no idea. I've not seen you for a good while, mind. Any road, congratulations, pal. An' call me Charlie, for goodness' sake. When did you get wed?"

"Just over a year since. Back last August."

I remember waiting for him to supply a little more information, not least his wife's name, but he seemed lost in his own thoughts. Perhaps he was simply tired; his face was smeared with the grime of a day's graft. I made to set about my journey, and he turned to join me. We strode on, side by side.

"So, what you doin' round here, any road?"

"I live in town now," he said, returning his attention to me.

"In Manchester?"

"Aye."

"So you finally left Hyde, then?"

"Aye, I did."

"You took my advice?"

"I suppose I did. Eventually."

He spoke quietly, measuring his words as though they might run dry at any moment.

"Where you livin', then, Danny?"

"Where? In town."

"Aye, you said. Whereabouts?"

"Back o' Peter Street. It's not so bad. Pretty central."

"An' you're workin' round here?"

"Aye. Aye I am."

"On the docks?"

"No. No, at Trafford Park. I did come for a job on the docks. You know, when I left Hyde. A job over at Salford." He stopped to turn his head briefly back in that direction. "I did start there. A couple o' year ago now. Maintenance, it were. Mainly on the cranes."

"But you're not there no more?"

"No, I'm at Westie's now. You know, Westinghouse."

"Oh, I know Westinghouse alright. It's a big employer these days, an' no mistake."

"Oh, aye, Sheds an' sheds of assembly lines an' workshops. It's all turbine production, generators an' such like. An' better wages."

"An' you deserve 'em, I'll bet. You're a bloody good mechanic, aren't you?"

"Well, they seem to think so."

"Good for you, Danny."

"Aye, I've no regrets."

"You got time for a drink? Fancy a glass o' beer?"

"Oh, I dunno. Happen not. Better not. Thanks all the same."

"You in a rush, then?"

"No. No, not really. But I do need to get back."

"You walk it back, do you?"

"No. No, it's too far away. It's a trek from Trafford Park to the station as it is."

"Aye, I suppose it is. Well, I'll walk with you to the station."

"You catchin' the train an' all?"

"No, I live round the corner."

"That's handy."

"Aye, I'm lucky. Isabella Street. You'll probably not know it."

"No."

"You'll have to come round one o' these days. Meet the family again. Bring Mrs Harrop along, an' all."

"Thanks, Mr Knott. Charlie. That'd be grand."

It was not far to the congested northbound platform at Old Trafford railway station. I found a Booth & Byrne business card in my pocket, pressed it into his hand and pointed out the telephone number. I insisted he contact me when he had some time to spare.

"If you dial that number you'll get our switchboard," I explained. "Ask for me an' then someone'll put you through to my own office device. It's a wonderful thing, the telephone, Danny. It's the future, believe you me."

We shook hands. I patted him on the back and watched him as he headed up the steps, bag of tools dangling from his hand, merging and then disappearing into the impatient crowd of passengers.

Isabella Street has altered a little since the time we bought our house there almost twenty years ago; not so much in its physical configuration, but certainly with regard to its inhabitants. Like the other streets that lie close to it, it has traditionally been populated by what might be called a professional class of worker: the families of educated men who earned a commensurate wage. In more recent years certain dwellings have been partitioned, offering units of rented accommodation for folk of lesser means. There are quite evidently a greater number of children to be seen.

Meanwhile the urban village of Old Trafford is really no more. The expansion of industry around the docks, notably the establishment of Trafford Park as what I have heard described as *the world's first industrial park*, has encouraged the building of cheap terraced housing and a shift in the social profile of this once bucolic corner of Stretford. To Ada's dismay the tennis club sold off its land and re-established itself in Didsbury, around ten miles to the south. She is thankful that the public courts in nearby Hullard Park are still in use. The open grassy spaces of Seymour Park remain, but the well-tended Royal Botanical Gardens have recently been redeveloped as a kind of amusement park, going by the name of White City. There is no escaping the fact that many more labourers' families are moving out of the centre of the city and into the area, in tandem with a plethora of shops and businesses that rely on their trade.

Perhaps one of the most significant developments has been the building of the large football ground on land to the south of Trafford Park, between the Bridgwater Canal and the railway lines. We watched in fascination as the great edifice went up throughout the year 1909. Built to accommodate eighty thousand spectators (surely an exaggerated number), it is referred to as a *stadium*; we know it as the United Football Ground. Its capacity dwarfs that of the county cricket ground which sits sedately in its park less than a mile away, and it is the new home of Manchester United, an established Football League club who had previously been playing on a much-maligned ground in the east of the city. Once a fortnight during the season, as the factories fall quiet, the streets around here are still abuzz with jostling throngs of young men. Loud, excited conversations float above the crunching of thousands of boots on the cobbles as the sounds and smells of a football crowd fill the Saturday afternoon air.

3

Mr Martyn Byrne, Chairman of the Board, Manchester man, was rarely seen in Cornbrook Road, preferring to govern the company from his offices in the city centre. He would say that the proximity of railway stations there gave him easy access to business meetings in Liverpool or Leeds or Birmingham. The ease of access to his substantial home in rural Cheshire was just as important, it was sometimes quietly said.

Whenever he did appear on our premises, always flanked by one bag-carrying factotum or other and usually accompanied by Mr Pollitt, the employees would seem slightly on edge; it felt like a classroom of schoolchildren being unexpectedly visited by an overbearing headmaster. I myself was not immune to this irrational anxiety, no matter how confident I was in my own work. I have to say that more oftentimes than not our collective unease was unwarranted. It was very likely that Mr Byrne would arrive, spend an hour or two in his office on the second floor and then disappear without a single word to his port-side staff. Seldom would he make a disparaging remark in public; more commonly he might dispense a casual word or two of encouragement or even praise.

His dealings with me were courteous and business-like, as I would expect them to be. He included me in meetings that had a relevance to the function I played in the company, and my opinions were listened to, at least superficially. Every year at Christmastime a bottle of Irish whiskey found its way on to my desk with a label around its neck bearing seasonal greetings, signed simply *Byrne*.

It was around the middle of summer when one day the chairman strode into my office unannounced, leaving his factotum hovering on the threshold.

"A word, Mr Knott?" he enquired, leaving me with no choice other than to put my ink pen to one side, remove my spectacles and give him my undivided attention.

"Mr Byrne. This is an unexpected pleasure."

"Are you free tomorrow evening?" he asked, batting aside my flattery.

I wondered where such a question might lead.

"Well, aye, I am." I replied, failing to disguise my hesitancy. "I'm sure I am."

It was an instinctively truthful answer, blind alley or not.

"Excellent. That's excellent."

He had approached the very edge of my desk. His whiskery face caught the light from my lamp. His brown leather belt was very tight around his middle. His preference to stand made for a short conversation.

"Then you are invited to dinner on Number Two Dock," he continued. "Actually, it's my invitation but I cannot attend. At short notice I am indisposed. I thought of asking Mr Pollitt, but his wife is unwell. Then I thought of Mr Aspinwall, but he's such a miserable old beggar, no good in company. Then I thought of you. It's the *Duchesse d'Aquitaine*. You'll be familiar with the ship?"

"I am, Mr Byrne. She sails at the end of the week."

"I believe so. As you know, we've been representing the line for years. Well, the captain's an old friend of mine. Puybonieux is his name."

He handed me a card with the details of the invitation, handwritten in a royal blue ink. I read the name, intrigued by the spelling which, from Byrne's pronunciation, I could hardly have guessed at.

"Jean-Jacques," he continued. "French, obviously. Quite a character. He'll treat you well, I'm quite sure of it. Always does. You'll eat well. It might not be what you're used to, Mr Knott, but you'll eat well, I can guarantee."

"I'm very much obliged, Mr Byrne. It's very kind o' you to think o'me."

"No bother. You're doing me a favour. And you will represent the company admirably, I've no doubt. Give the captain my apologies, won't you?"

Without waiting for a response, he turned and left the room, and I heard two pairs of footsteps briskly crossing the office floor, then fade away.

The *Duchesse d'Aquitaine* was indeed a name I was aware of but I had never before set foot aboard. I had been processing her exportation docket the previous afternoon: a steam-powered merchant ship of moderate dimensions, she had arrived from Genoa in Italy, calling at her home port of Bordeaux on the way before docking in Manchester with a cargo of fruits and footwear, wine and olive oil, and several tonnes of quarried marble. Now she was to be laden with coal and machinery and equipment for the Italian railways. Of Captain Puybonieux I knew nothing at all, but that was soon to change.

Ada advised, nay insisted, that I wore my smartest suit and a high collar and necktie. She picked out a Dooley's powder blue one in silk, a birthday gift from her parents as I recall.

"The French like things in blue," she said with some authority.

Whether they do or do not, the captain made no comment on my appearance. As for my host, he wore a dinner jacket with such insouciance he might have been born in it. He received me in the ship's private quarters with great charm: a short man of about my age, with bright brown eyes in a weather-beaten face, and with what remained of his hair cropped close to his skull.

The meal was served in a small, simply-furnished dining room. We sat around a circular table that took up most of the space and at the centre of which was set a silver candelabra holding three newly-lit candles whose shimmering light cast shadows of us all into the recesses. Watching over us like an indulgent mother was the face of a lady framed in a small oil painting which hung on a wall: the portrait of a woman of means from a time long ago, a tiara set upon her chestnut hair, a benign smile on her lips. Noticing my interest, Puybonieux identified her for me as Eleanor of Aquitaine, who, he remarked, was both Queen of France and Queen of England in her eventful life.

"And she was the mother of Richard Coeur de Lion, as I'm sure you know," he reminded us all, and, directing his attention towards me, added: "Lionheart, as you would call him. The painting is not of that time, of course. It's *Flamand*, Flemish, early seventeenth century. Simply a representation."

We others found ourselves nodding in wordless agreement.

There were only five of us for dinner, which, to be honest, I found to be a relief. Puybonieux's first mate joined us, as did the ship's doctor, a Parisian with a neatly trimmed beard who spoke very good English. I was also introduced to a representative of the Cooperative Wholesale Society, a youngish fellow from Bolton by the name of Brocklebank, who knew the captain from previous meetings.

It was a jolly affair. A young waiter served glasses of wine – a choice of red or white. From the start Puybonieux was at the centre of it all, clearly enjoying the attention of an audience; one minute he was offering a serious opinion on European trading patterns, the next he was playing devil's advocate with a twinkle in his eye simply to spice up the conversation. Beyond his quarters and the galley below, the ship appeared to be quite empty of crew. The men had been sent ashore, he informed us, to get a proper taste of Salford: the unpalatable food, the dreadful beer and the delightful young women.

At the start of the meal we were served with half a yellow orange sitting in a bowl. I followed Brocklebank's lead with a small spoon, scooping out the segments of pink flesh from its skin. It had a taste I did not recognise: to my palate a mix of the flavours of an orange and a lemon. It was tart yet quite delicious.

"It is a grapefruit, Mr Knott," explained the captain, who had been observing the curiosity in my expression.

"A grapefruit? Oh, so *this* is a grapefruit?" I wondered aloud. "I've never seen one cut open before. Well, it hardly tastes like grapes, I must say."

Both Puybonieux and the doctor were already smiling: firstly to each other and then in my direction.

"What we have is an example of the irrationality of the English language, Mr Knott," stated the captain. "And you are right to notice it. The fruit bears no resemblance at all to a grape. We call it *pamplemousse*."

I nodded, setting another segment on to my tongue.

"*Pamplemousse*," he repeated, the smile fixed on his face. "Say it, Mr Knott. Say the word, please. Slowly, slowly."

"Pawm-pler-moose," I said, and then again, more slowly. "Pawm-pler-moose."

It was a lovely word, round and luscious on the tongue, as juicy as the fruit itself.

"Remember it," added Puybonieux, "the next time you find one."

I was told that the ship's cook was an Italian, a Genoese, just as a dish of *spaghetti* was carried in and set before us. This too was new to me: thin strands of a soft wheat-based *pasta* (as it was explained), under a serving of a sauce of minced beef and tomato, flavoured with what I imagine were Mediterranean herbs. One by one the young waiter expertly served a portion on to our dishes. I relished the food but it was by no means straightforward to eat. I found no knife to cut the *pasta*; instead, I observed my fellow guests using large spoons to set a tangle of the stuff upon with a skilled twist of the fork.

"This is a game," Brocklebank said to me under his breath. "I too was served this dish on my first visit. It's a test. They love to laugh at the English."

He had already tucked his napkin into the collar so that it covered his shirtfront. I followed his example.

"Very wise," commented the captain. "A beginner like you will otherwise end the evening with a lovely blue tie covered in *ragù*."

I did not make as much of a fool of myself as he probably would have liked. The doctor complimented me on my dexterity but he may well have been joking. I was the last to finish by some distance; my napkin looked like a scene from Waterloo but beneath it my shirt and tie were spotless and my efforts were toasted with further glasses of claret.

The conversation drifted on to the subjects of travel, of sailing, of the delights of the Mediterranean climate. The first mate was of Spanish origin – his English was hard to follow – whereas the surgeon was an Anglophile: gently stroking his beard, he told us that some of his happiest holidays as a child had been spent on the island of Guernsey.

"It was a favourite place of my parents. They loved it for the peace and the gentle climate. As for us children, we were just happy to be by the sea. It was just the ticket."

His use of that outworn phrase made me smile. This was the second time the surgeon had used the expression. Earlier in the evening he had thus described a second helping of *spaghetti alla bolognese*. Just the ticket. I guessed it was an idiom he had recently learned and was keen to try out in the company of Englishmen.

Meanwhile, Brocklebank remained tight-lipped on the subject of foreign travel and I too had little to offer beyond experiences on the Lancashire coast.

Later on, a platter of cheeses was brought to the table and a bottle of port appeared. I say "cheeses", but I recognised none of them as examples of cheese as an Englishman might describe it. Brocklebank, as an executive of a large-scale grocery business, was a step ahead of me, able not only to name them all but also to add a description of what I might expect from a sample of each. A pale, flat disc, the size of a bread and butter plate, with a dried skin around its edges, was heartily recommended. I watched my compatriot slice a triangular piece, and then everybody else's eyes settled on me as I followed his example.

"*C'est du Camembert*," said Puybonieux proudly. "It is our classic French cheese. Please, taste it."

I found the crust unpleasant and, once broken, the interior was soft and yellow and runny like the yolk of a boiled egg. The taste was sour and the smell was worse: a pungent tang of decay. I did not describe it thus aloud but I dare say my face betrayed my displeasure.

"I admit that this example is more mature than ideal," said the captain, helping himself from the platter. "I think this one has been on board for over two weeks. Nevertheless, to a connoisseur, the richer the flavour the better."

"I will never be a connoisseur, captain," I smiled, taking a mouthful of port to wash away the taste.

"Well, at least our cheeses do have flavour," he went on, to nods of agreement from the Frenchmen at the table.

"Have you tried our Cheshire?" I asked. "Unbeatable, I'd say."

"Only by a fine Lancashire," suggested Brocklebank.

"A creamy taste," I continued, ignoring him. "A crumbly texture, salty an' sweet at the same time. Very fine."

"I have eaten it once, *monsieur*. The English say 'mild'. I'd say *sans goût* – quite tasteless."

"But have you eaten it grilled – meltin' under a flame?" I added, wishing I could conjure a sample for him out of thin air.

"Oh, we don't need to burn our cheeses to give them flavour, Mr Knott! It is a pity that the Camembert does not please you. I can see that what they say is true after all: the people of Manchester are not so *sophistiqué* as our friends in Liverpool."

"Sophisticated, in Liverpool?" I spluttered. "I don't think those two words should ever be spoken in the same sentence!"

The doctor was grinning.

"*Monsieur, je vous taquine!*" said the captain.

"He's teasing you," said Brocklebank.

Suddenly all my dining companions were laughing. I emptied my glass, sat back in my chair and laughed along with them.

The evening ended with Puybonieux regaling us with a little of his family history. He was related to the Emperor Napoleon, he claimed: he had a great cousin who was married to one of the Bonapartes.

"I should have been a soldier," he mused. "Probably a general. Not a poor sailor ferrying grapefruits to England."

He let his thoughts drift off into the fug of tobacco smoke, leaving the rest of us in a kind of sympathetic silence, but I think we all knew it was a pantomime.

"Of course, he was talking nonsense," said Brocklebank, as together we descended the gangplank shortly before midnight. "He does that a lot, Jean-Jacques, you'll have noticed. Talk nonsense. He just can't help himself. The last time I was on board he swore to us his wife was a descendant of William the Conqueror."

Each of us was carrying a cloth bag of gifts from the galley. In my case a couple of grapefruits, a bottle of wine and a boxed Camembert cheese.

"Let your wife try it, Mr Knott," Puybonieux had said, unexpectedly embracing me as we took our leave. "I have no doubt she has a more refined palate than you do."

Whether or not the captain of the *Duchesse d'Aquitaine* could justifiably call himself a quasi-Bonaparte, he was proved to be accurate in his estimation of my wife's liking for the Camembert. It appeared on a dinner plate one afternoon, in the middle of the kitchen table, unboxed and odorous, just as I was making myself a more orthodox cheese sandwich. Alfred joined us, cut himself a chunk and tasted it: immediately he declared it to be delicious. Ada was already savouring a second helping.

She has since bought more of it from time to time; it's a question of finding such a rarity in the shops. It must be said that there are a few modern groceries springing up in the smarter districts of the city which cater for a more discerning clientele. For our unbreakable English class system is based on much more than ancestry and property and the way a chap might talk; it manifests itself quite shamelessly in a woman's choice of gloves, in her hairstyle and, most obvious of all, in her shopping list.

I believe Ada did genuinely enjoy eating the stuff. As for my son's blatant shunning of my offer to share the cheese sandwich, it was of a piece with his sarcastic usage of one of my (apparently annoying) expressions, when he declared,

51

even imitating my accent: *Camembert cheese, father – it's the future*. At the time it struck me as just one more instance of his adolescent contrariness.

4

Months passed before I bumped into Daniel Harrop again. On this occasion I persuaded him to join me for a drink.

At the junction of Cornbrook Road and Chester Road I spotted him loping along the pavement in the evening gloom, his head covered in a hood, his eyes fixed on the damp flagstones which shone silvery in the reflected light of the streetlamps. Hard rain had fallen through the day but had stopped at around tea time. It must have been about half past six.

I called his name across the street but there were carriages passing between us and my voice failed to carry. I waited for the traffic to move on and darted over to the opposite pavement to catch up with him.

"Danny, is that you?" I asked, touching his shoulder.

He spun round in alarm.

"Sorry to startle you," I said. "How are you?"

He stopped to take me in, looking me up and down as if I were a stranger.

"Oh, Mr Knott, it's you," he mumbled. "I were in me own world. I didn't recognise you in the dark."

"You've missed your train tonight, have you?"

"No. Not really. I've taken to walkin' more often than not."

"Even on dreary nights in November?"

"Oh, that dunna bother me."

"You finishin' later these days?"

"Aye, I've been doin' extra shifts since September."

"You'll be rakin' it in."

He smiled ruefully, then turned to resume his walk into town.

"Are you in a hurry?" I asked, taking a hold of his sleeve.

"Well…"

"How about a drink? I'm payin'. I've had a bugger of a day an' there'll be nobody at home till later. There's a pub round the corner."

Danny appeared hesitant, moved his weight from one foot to the other.

"Aye, go on, then," he said, an affirmative that did surprise me.

"Good lad," I said, patting him on the back. "Come on. Follow me. Let's get a seat somewhere warm. An' I'm Charlie, remember. *Mr Knott*'s for them at work."

The Full Tun was a small ale house situated at the end of a dark side-street. I had been inside several times before with colleagues from the office, and although its trappings were basic, I found the atmosphere convivial and the beer was well maintained. Groups of men were drinking together at the bar but the room was not busy. I bought two glasses of ale and fetched them to a table by the hearth where Danny had found some seats. He thanked me, we clinked glasses and drank. A feeble fire was flickering and in its yellow light I noticed the fellow's cheekbone was bruised.

He declined my offer of a cigarette. I had almost forgotten the impression I had formed some years before about Daniel Harrop: he was a reserved man often lost in his own thoughts. Nothing had changed, it seemed. Beyond banalities it was hard to draw much conversation from him. He showed little curiosity about my own circumstances; perhaps they were not so remarkable after all.

"How's married life?" I asked at one point.

"What do you mean?" came the response.

"Well, how's it goin'? What do you like to do together?" I regretted broaching the subject. "Sorry, what's her name again, your missus?"

"Flora."

"Flora. That's nice. Does she go out to work, your Flora?"

"Good God, no," he snorted.

"You must have a neat an' tidy house, then," I said, "if she's at home all day. An' a nice meal waitin' for you, I expect."

Danny laughed. A dismissive laugh, I thought.

"Flora likes to spend her own time on herself," he said at length. "An' there's nowt wrong with that, I dunna suppose."

I sipped my beer, letting him carry on at his own steady pace:

"She's good company. She likes her shoppin' – shoppin' for clothes, I mean – an' her theatre, an' her concerts. An' then there's her visitin'. She's got quite a gang o' friends. Women friends. What she calls her circle."

He laughed again. I waited for him to elaborate but he took up his glass and drank thirstily from it, bringing an end to the subject.

We each had a second glass which I insisted on paying for. There was no question that Danny would not be sitting under the low ceiling of the Full Tun had I not invited him to join me.

I remembered that he shared his step-father's love of football and so I introduced the subject, even though I knew I would have little to contribute. Happily, it proved to be a more fruitful topic of conversation. Danny still played the game. He told me with a self-deprecating smile that at his time of life he now found himself chasing after young lads half his age, but he could still handle himself and enjoyed taking part. He played most weekends for a chapel team in Salford.

"We play against other churches, pub sides, works teams," he explained. "There's a league we're in."

"Are you any good?"

"Oh, you know, we win a few, lose a few. We've just had a lad join us who played a couple o' games for Manchester City. Well, their reserve side, any road. He had a niggly injury an' they let him go."

"You've got a match this week, have you?"

"Aye, we have. We're playin' in Eccles."

"That's quite a way."

"No, it's not so far, Charlie. An' we've got a match comin' up near where you live, if I'm not mistaken. Stretford St John's. Next month. A week or two before Christmas."

"Well, I'll have to come an' watch you."

"We dunna get too many speccies. A bloke an' 'is dog, that kind o' thing."

"I'll bring my lad. Our Alfred. He likes his football. You'll have to let me know when it is."

"Aye, alright."

"You still 'ave my telephone number at work?"

"Aye, somewhere."

"Well, then."

"Aye, I'll let you know."

Before we parted I could not restrain myself from asking about his swollen cheekbone. He laughed, cursed his clumsiness and told a brief tale about an accident with a pulley chain at the factory. He thanked me for the beer, declined a third and had fastened up his coat before I finished my second cigarette and stood to collect up our glasses. The pub was filling up with regulars, including some men, I guessed, who had already been home for their tea and a change of shirt, and had come there to meet their pals to drink and chatter and play cards together. We walked out into the dark street and after a cursory handshake Danny was gone, quite evidently keen to continue his journey home without further ado.

Although he had never met Daniel, Alfred was curious enough to see his football team play, especially as we could easily walk to the pitch where St John's held their matches.

It was true that if my son spoke of sport at all, it was football rather than cricket that he might mention. I play cricket very rarely these days but had taken part regularly well into my forties, finding church teams in the area who were happy to engage my services. In my youth I would rattle down wicket after wicket with pure pace: ten per cent technique and ninety per cent brute force. But those days were over. For a start, my slowly expanding girth did not much lend itself to sprinting. Instead, I had managed to develop a style of swing bowling that I found successful off a more sedate run-up. Occasionally a club I attached myself to would have a junior team and I encouraged Alfred to take up the sport. As an eleven- and twelve-year-old he was tall for his age and soon learned to bowl a decent fast one. His love of playing was fickle, however. *There's too much standing around*, he would say. *The games go on too long. I've got schoolwork to do. My back's aching again after last weekend.* I tried to hide my disappointment but probably did not try hard enough, and so cricket became another subject over which we argued. For most of the time Ada sensibly kept her distance.

In the weeks that followed I heard no confirmation from Danny, but in the meantime I made my own enquiries at the church, where one of the sidesmen happened to be a book-keeper with Booth & Byrne. Indeed there was a match scheduled for Saturday afternoon of December 6th.

It was a bright, cold day as Alfred and I set off for the recreation field, ready to take in the fresh air and be entertained by some amateur athletic endeavour. The game was a rumbustious affair, ending in a victory for the hosts by four goals to three, which provided many a moment of amusement. We watched twenty-two energetic footballers give their all to the occasion but were somewhat puzzled, if not disappointed, that at no point did Daniel Harrop appear amongst them.

Part Three
1914 - 15

1

If I had not been such an avid reader of a daily newspaper, I could have probably lived through the weeks of late summer and early autumn without realising that our country was at war with Germany. It was a fact that there were somewhat fewer ships plying their trade along the canal but the dwindling was so very gradual and at first was comparable to a seasonal fluctuation. And the absence of young men from the factories and the docksides was barely noticeable in those sultry days. One immediate impact, however, was that plans for an expansion of Salford Docks – a Number Ten Dock – were abandoned. Meanwhile, food was still in good supply, stocks of fuel remained adequate and people I knew still grumbled about work, made jokes behind their bosses' backs and gossiped about their neighbours well before conversations might ever turn to the conflict on the European continent.

Besides which, there were other stories in the newspapers. On a local note, for example, I read of a theft of rifles and ammunition from the garrison at Chester Castle, headquarters of the Cheshire Regiment. I always kept an eye on the county cricket scores. There was more alarming news of arson attacks and other such vandalism by members of the suffragettes, and the tribulations of Mr Asquith's government in granting Irish Home Rule rumbled on in the background. By August, however, it was clear that the newspapers were devoting more and more space to stories with an international flavour.

The assassination of an unknown Austrian aristocrat, the bellicose reaction of the German-speaking nations, the simmering resentments and generations-long hatreds rising to the surface like an erupting volcano – it all seemed very remote from the day-to-day routines of Isabella Street, of Pomona Docks, of Booth & Byrne. And yet our nation *was* at war, a part of a Triple Entente engaged with a Triple Alliance. Declarations of war had followed declarations of war like rapid exchanges in a lethal game of draughts. Bombs and bullets in Belgium were echoing in Berlin and Paris and, of course, in London too. But not so much closer to home, it seemed. It seemed that way to me, at least.

2

It was no surprise that Mr Horridge was to be released. He had taken to shouting down the telephone line, unconvinced that the machine could transmit his voice down a wire over a distance of several miles. He was disturbing the rest of the accounts team; indeed, there were times when his screaming could be heard on the upper floors of the building, including in my own office. Mr Dewsbury and his favourite junior colleague Mr South, both members of my first-floor staff, were merciless in teasing him. They placed telephone calls to the device on the ground floor, insisting, in disguised voices, to speak to Mr Horridge. On one occasion there was an employee of the General Post Office standing on the pavement outside the building with a parcel for him, demanding a signature. Horridge grumpily exited the premises to find no such employee. On another, Mr South, pretending to be Mr Byrne's personal assistant, told Mr Horridge that Mr Byrne himself wanted to speak to him. *Would he hold the receiver a moment, please, while the connection was made?* The connection was left unmade, of course, but Horridge was left hanging on, muttering to himself, for the best part of half an hour. The funniest incident (although far be it from me to condone such puerile shenanigans from my professional staff) ended with Mr Horridge shouting the word "sex" at the top of his voice over and over again, causing great amusement among those at the ground-floor desks. This time Mr Dewsbury was a technician from the telephone company, calling to test the clarity of the line.

"Please, sir, could you call out, in your clearest voice, the numbers one to ten?"

Rather reluctantly, Horridge duly did as he was told while Mr South padded down the stairs to observe the fun.

"Thank you, sir. That sounded absolutely fine. One more thing, if I may. To test a different frequency range, phonemes of the German language are recommended. Could I ask you to repeat after me the same numbers in German?"

"I don't know any German," Horridge was heard to complain.

"No, no, it doesn't matter, sir. Simply repeat them after me. As clearly as you can, sir. *Eins...zwei...drei...*"

"*Eins, zwei, drei...*"

"*Vier...fünf...sechs...*"

"*Vier, fünf, sechs...*"

"Sorry, sir, I didn't quite catch the last one..."

"*Sechs.*"

"A little louder, please, sir."

"*Sechs!*"

"And again, if you don't mind..."

"Oh, for goodness' sake... *Sechs! Sechs! Sechs!*"

He really was an old curmudgeon, at his happiest, so they said, forty years earlier when he worked as a dapper office boy at one of the Salford brickworks. He had been a young man once. Now he was a desiccated grouch that the future had left behind. I was touched that he made a special journey upstairs to my office to shake me by the hand and thank me personally for my support over the years of our collaboration. Racking my brains, I could think of nothing I had done beyond basic civility to help him in his duties. I had had disputes with many colleagues, including those at Booth

& Byrne, but I had kept Horridge at arm's length, preferring to refer matters of finance to one of his more enterprising juniors.

Osmund Porritt told me the news of the retirement, "a nudged exit, an encouraged departure", on one of his regular visits to Pomona. Mr Porritt had his own office on the second floor, a grand, almost luxurious space which he had the run of. Strictly speaking it was Mr Byrne's Pomona office, but our chairman was a rare visitor.

It was to this upper chamber, whose large windows allowed a flood of bright January sunlight, that I was summoned one morning not so long after the New Year holiday.

With a smouldering cigarette pinched between his fingers, Mr Porritt remained seated behind the polished oak desk, but another man, a young fellow I did not recognise, stood to greet me as I entered. He wore a fashionable worsted suit, a cream-coloured collar and a spotted necktie, and below a thick wave of russet brown hair his handsome face was dominated by a pair of sparkling green eyes.

"This is Mr Mulloy," announced Mr Pollitt.

The man took a step towards me, offered a wide, closed smile and a firm hand to shake.

"He will be joining us in accounts," continued the managing director. "More or less in Mr Horridge's old role. At least in the medium term."

"Pleased to meet you," said the younger man.

"Pleased to meet you, Mr Mulloy," I replied, returning the smile.

"Sit, please, the pair of you," said Mr Pollitt. "Mr Knott here is an experienced hand in our company. He basically runs our operations here at the docks, the day-to-day management of shipping arrangements and so on. You will have your own support in the accounts division, Mr Mulloy, but any questions you have about what goes on here and how you can best contribute to the process, I suggest you avail yourself of Mr Knott's wealth of knowledge."

And then addressing me:

"Mr Mulloy comes to us from our office in Liverpool. And he comes with excellent references. I trust you will offer your support to him, Mr Knott – help him find his feet, as it were. Especially in the early weeks of his time with us."

"Of course," I said, adding an abrupt nod.

Had I noticed a Liverpudlian twang in the man's voice in his brief greeting? I certainly noticed it during the conversation we had once we had been released from the upper sanctum. Mr Mulloy was already on his way out of the room when Mr Pollitt called me back.

"Charlie, how's the family?" he asked, suddenly adjusting the dialogue into our out-of-office mode.

"Everyone seems happy enough. No dramas beyond the usual. Our Alfred's set his heart on writin'. You remember, they took him on at the *Courier*."

"Yes, you did mention it."

"An' your two, Osmund?"

"Yes, well. Where do I start? The latest is they want to move out. Together, I mean. Understandable, I suppose, but they'll be expecting me to pay for everything. They don't want a little flat in Didsbury, though, do they? They have a plan. They're on about setting up a boarding house by the seaside."

"Are they?"

"Have you heard of Cleveleys?"

"Near Blackpool?"

"That's the place. North of Blackpool. Quite refined. Which means expensive. They must think I'm made of money!"

"It could be a good investment, Osmund."

"That's as maybe, but what they've got their eyes on is out of my reach. I don't know, your children never let you rest in peace, do they?"

"You worry about 'em the same whether they're nine or nineteen."

"Or thirty-five-year-old twins in my case! Anyway," he said, nodding towards the open door, "you've got another one to keep an eye on now, Charlie. Young Mr Mulloy. I don't expect he'll cause you too much bother, mind. He seems like a grand lad."

The new employee had grown up in Kirkdale, an area of Liverpool, as he explained, where the sights and sounds and smells of the activity of the Merseyside docks were never far away. His father had been a docker since the age of fifteen. His older brother worked for the Port Authority on the pilot boats. The fellow standing before me was thirty-one years old, unmarried, and had plans to make his fortune in the world of finance before he found himself a wife. He made no secret that he viewed the accounts department of Booth & Byrne as a stepping stone to a position in one of the more important banking houses in Manchester. For all his self-confidence I found him neither arrogant nor conceited. To tell the truth, I saw a little of my younger self in his spirit. I too had been impatient to jump from one job to the next, striving for a post I deemed worthy of my talents.

The company had secured rented accommodation for him in a pair of rooms in a large partitioned house in Ordsall, no more than a ten-minute walk through the narrow streets from his new place of work. I visited him in his rooms on two occasions over the next few weeks. He had little need of me professionally in spite of Osmund Pollitt's concern, but he was a friendly sort and I did like to listen to his amusing observations of our colleagues, served with a spiky sense of humour and all expressed, to my ears at least, in his unusual accent. We quickly dispensed with hierarchy and the formality of surnames; in truth I never considered myself to be his boss. Just as I was happy to be called Charlie, he insisted that I address him, not as Sidney, but rather as did all his friends back in Kirkdale, simply as Mull.

I offered to take him to watch a match at my old cricket club when the summer came, or even to a game at the county ground. After all, Liverpudlian and Mancunian, we were all Lancastrians, weren't we?

"Sorry, my friend," I remember him replying, "cricket's not for me. I played a bit of football as a kid, but I gave that up once I grew out of short pants. I was never that good in any case. I had more success with the young ladies than I ever did with a leather ball, if you know what I mean."

He winked at me and lit a cigarette.

"That was the sort of scorin' I'd sooner be doin.'"

I had to laugh. There was a crudity to his language which was disarmed by his nonchalance.

"There's a lass at the moment, by the way, Charlie."

"Oh, aye?"

"A belter."

"Back in Liverpool?"

"No. No, she's here alright. I saw her last night."

"Tell me more, Mull."

"She works in town. On the switchboard – what does she call it? – the switch. The switch at London Road railway station. In the main offices. Well, she's got the voice for it, that's a fact. A proper nice voice. What you'd call cultured. Not like yours, eh? An' what a looker, Charlie. Absolutely gorgeous, she is. Prettiest one I've met in a long while, I can tell you that for nothin'. An' the way she walks! Well, really, she should be on a stage. In a theatre show, really, she should. Mind you, happen not. There'd be too many oglin' eyes. I wanna keep her to myself."

He stopped talking to take a long drag of his cigarette, and to give me time to let his words settle in my mind.

"What's she called, this rare beauty?"

"Violet. Like the flower. Like the little blue flower."

"Violet. Well, it sounds like you're a lucky lad."

"Aye, an' she's a lucky lass," he said with a grin as wide as the Mersey.

3

By the spring of 1915 the effects of war were starting to be felt in Manchester. Although the Royal Navy had disabled most of the German battle cruisers, shipping (and therefore trade) remained at the mercy of the submarine attacks in the North Atlantic: here was an enemy that was difficult to trace and nearly impossible to predict. Safe shipping routes were critical to maintain the supply to our shores of food, raw cotton, oil, rubber, metals and so on. Suddenly, it seemed, the routes we relied on could not be effectively protected; ships were targeted by torpedoes, many were lost, their crew and commodities never reaching intended ports like ours.

The Port Authority estimated a ten per cent annual reduction in volume of imports by the April of that year. As the operations manager of a shipping agent, I was well placed to record a similar drop in exports. Booth & Byrne was a well-established company with excellent contacts in local commerce and, as such, we were not short of business: no worker was laid off at this time. Wages remained stable even though there was noticeably less in the shops to spend money on. Here and there shelves were beginning to empty, and to stay empty. According to Ada, who searched high and low, neither grapefruits nor French cheeses were to be found any more.

Meanwhile, the land war looked to be bogged down in a stalemate. The German advances in Belgium and north-eastern France had been halted and both sides had dug mile after mile of trenches to fortify their positions. Special war correspondents were in the midst of it all, and news reached home quickly: I would read about a battle only a day or two after it had begun. Everyone was alarmed at how what had started in the Balkans less than a year earlier had spread to Russia, to the Ottoman Empire and to North Africa. The newspapers provided some geographic detail but I found myself consulting the outsized plates of a world atlas that we had in our offices. I was looking for places like Picardy and Lorraine, Sebastopol and Gallipoli. Before long the conflict had extended further: to the Middle East, to colonial Africa, even to the Pacific Ocean. For myself, a man who had never set foot outside the north-west of England, it was an education, and a most harrowing one at that.

From a fairly young age I had an interest in British politics and especially the unjust exclusion of the working man from any meaningful influence on them. I was no firebrand, however; indeed, the Chartist rebels of the previous century would put me to shame in their readiness to grasp the nettle. Nonetheless, impatience with the rate of progress towards equality was embedded in my character and I suppose it still is to a lesser extent. I was quick to anger and reacted badly towards small-mindedness and incompetence from those in authority.

Gazing at a map of Europe I was aware how parochial my politics had become. I never joined a trades union but instead nailed my colours to the mast of the fledgling Labour Party, which seemed to me to offer a more direct route to providing representation for the labouring classes, at least in parliament if not yet in government. From a couple of M.P.s in 1900, at the general election of 1910 their number had swelled to forty-two, and districts of Manchester were indeed represented. Any sense of optimism was dealt a blow by the war: the party split into camps opposing or supporting the conflict. In my case I was guided by my principles: I shared Mr MacDonald's view that socialism was an international ideal, and that the war was being fought on the terms of the privileged classes as they postured across the European continent. It was a minority view, of course, and Mr MacDonald resigned as leader of the party the moment the war on Germany was declared.

My wife Ada is much more of an activist than I ever was. She is fortunate in her circumstances: her father was a wealthy businessman, she was well educated and has never wanted for anything material. She reads voraciously and debates quite lethally. Her passion is the struggle for the right of women to vote; her fury is aimed at the injustice and stupidity that prevents the British female from shaping our parliament. It was a fight that was halted in the main due to the distraction of the war. The members of the Women's Social and Political Union, namely Mrs Pankhurst's suffragettes, turned much of their attention to the patriotic effort, helping to enable women into jobs, previously deemed unsuitable, that had been vacated by men dispatched abroad. Here too the picture was complicated: for example, Mrs Pankhurst's own daughter Sylvia was a pacifist, believing that if women could not vote then they should not support the fighting.

Political discussions were not unusual in our home. After a day in the office, attempting to avoid the inane ramblings of Mr Dewsbury and others, it was a pleasure to engage in a challenging conversation over a meal. To my disappointment, Alfred was oftentimes less disposed to contributing.

"Have you no opinions, son?" I would ask him, in fractious humour. "Is your mother right? Or am I? Speak up, lad!"

"I don't really care," he might say, pushing away his empty plate and making to leave the table. To my mind, it was the very worst thing he could say.

"You don't really care? Your country is at war, an' workin' men, young men, men your age, are dyin' on battlefields across Europe because the rich, entitled elites have decided the map of empires needs redrawin'…"

"Leave him, Charlie," Ada would say with a shake of the head. "Alfred's not always in the mood for a debate every time he sits down for his tea."

"Exactly," he would say. "Exactly that."

He would rise and push his chair under the table.

"There are other things going on, Father, you know."

And he would be gone – into the parlour, or up to his bedroom to write, or out to the back for a cigarette in the failing light.

I had tried my best with Alfred. I loved him, of course, but I did not always understand him. He was not at all how I had imagined a son of mine would turn out. That he gravitated to his mother was no surprise: as he was growing up, my work took so much of my time and practically all my energy. He was more interested in books and music than sport, and, in any case, it seemed that my attempts to teach him to play cricket had only pushed him towards a preference for football. My hopes that he follow a clerical route into business were thwarted when he announced that he wished to be a journalist or a playwright.

At the age of twenty he was already balancing both and yet earning a pittance. He was employed as an apprentice reporter with *The Manchester Courier*. I disapproved on two counts: it was a failing publication with dwindling sales, and its proprietors had always been staunch supporters of the establishment. Meanwhile his spare time spent at the Gaiety Theatre brought him a good deal of pleasure, I dare say, but he was no more than a volunteer. I once told him he was wasting his time writing scenes for plays that would never be performed.

"You'd do better writin' letters to companies askin' for a well-paid job."

It was one of the many facetious statements I now regret.

"An' you've taken to writin' poetry, your mother tells me. Poetry? What's that goin' to do for your prospects, then?"

"It's not poetry," he had snapped. "It's a lyric."

"A lyric?"

"A lyric for a song that's part of the play. So, it's not exactly poetry, is it? If you're wanting to demean me, Father, at least get your facts right."

The anger I felt at that remark was aimed more at myself than at my son, who had already left the room.

"Alfred's not like you, Charlie," said his mother once. "He doesn't have your impatience. He's a more whimsical soul."

"Whimsical?"

"He's young, he wants to have fun. Let him be light-hearted while he has the chance."

"So, he's not like you, neither, Ada."

"Oh, but he is. At that age. At that lovely, wide-eyed age. When I was twenty, I had no idea who the Prime Minister was. I'd never heard of the likes of Emmeline Pankhurst."

She stood and moved over to where I was sitting, a napkin at my throat, half a glass of beer at my hand.

"All I wanted to do at twenty was to try on all the new dresses at my father's shop," she continued. "And read novels, play the piano, write a little poetry."

I recalled the time I had made a joke about her name. Over recent years she had regularly chosen to keep the peace between me and my son by mediating, by becoming a gently-spoken umpire. I had come up with the nickname "Ada the Me-dee-Ada".

"If you want to be clever with words, Charlie, then go away and think of a better way to say sorry to your son," she had said, cutting me into pieces.

Now she was standing behind me, letting her arms fall around my neck. I sensed that she was smiling. I touched her hand and felt the rings on her wedding finger. She was right, of course. At twenty I was no different. All I cared about was playing cricket and earning money and chasing a pretty face. Educating myself on a diet of radical literature came a little later.

"I just wish he took things a bit more seriously," I said softly.

"It'll come," said Ada. "He's a good boy. He'll become a good man."

I felt her kiss the top of my head and tenderly squeezed her fingers in response.

4

Sidney Mulloy was good at his job. I knew a few of the fellows on the ground floor and they confirmed to me privately that the Liverpudlian had actually galvanised the accounts division by both his abilities and his personality. He had gained respect in quick order and was popular: he had both a serious work ethic and a sense of humour. Meanwhile he seemed drawn to me and I to him. If the opportunity arose he would leave his desk and ask to accompany me on any business I might have off the premises. He was eager to meet officers at the Port Authority, for example, or the Custom House. He liked to listen in as an observer to my conversations with representatives of shipping lines or local exporters of textiles or machinery. Afterwards he would have his own insights to share with me, all the while acknowledging my own role in negotiations with genuine appreciation.

Sometimes we would delay our return to Cornbrook Road to find an ale house to sit in and continue our dialogue in comfort. Once we had exhausted the topic of international trade, we might turn to the war – a subject he was always willing to discuss. He was a patriot, he insisted, which meant that he supported the decisions of His Majesty's government. He listened to my more cynical point of view with amusement.

"Why've you not signed up?" I asked him once. "Taken your King's shillin' an' joined a regiment? I'm sure the Manchester Pals would have you."

"Oh, I don't think I'm cut out for that, Charlie," he said.

"No? You don't fancy gettin' shot at if you poke your head

out of a trench in some bombed-out cabbage patch in northern France, then?"

He smiled and offered me a cigarette.

"Sorry to say, but I wouldn't know what to do with a rifle."

"They'll train you up, I dare say."

"I'm really not that courageous."

We lit our cigarettes and took a drag.

"But I applaud every man who is there," he continued after a moment. "An' I'd not undermine what they're doin'."

"I'm not underminin' 'em, Mull," I said. "I'm just angry that it's them that's dyin' and sufferin' for the decisions of a few old men in London."

We were on easier ground on personal matters. He was keen to meet Ada and Alfred. Without fail he was effusive in his admiration for Violet.

"You've got to meet her, Charlie!" he said many a time before an arrangement was finally made for the pair of them to visit Isabella Street. "There's plenty of nice lasses around here, but I think she's the one. I really do."

I was almost as excited as he was to hear him speak of her, and see his eyes light up each time he uttered her name.

On the first occasion I invited Mull to eat with us after work, Ada was instantly smitten by the fellow's good looks. I could not imagine a woman who might not be; indeed, a man less confident than me might have been anxious about his wife's fidelity. She was also struck by his enthusiasm for Violet.

"And where did you meet this angel?" she asked him.

He smiled and took a breath; of course, he had been expecting a question of this sort.

"Believe it or believe it not," he began, "I first set eyes on her in a clothes shop. A ladies' clothes shop, at that. One of those smart ones in town. I was lookin' for a gift for our Lily. My kid sister. Her twenty-first birthday. I was in this fancy shop on Cross Street…"

"Cross Street?" interrupted Ada. "It wasn't Dooley's, was it?"

"Dooley's? Aye, that was the shop. I'd not noticed the name – well, you don't really, do you? – but Violet recalls it whenever we talk about that day. It's her favourite shop in town, so she says."

"Dooley's, that's my father's shop. He owns it."

"Is that a fact, Mrs Knott?"

"Come along, you must call me Ada. Ada Dooley, as was. But Ada will do."

He declared there and then to the pair of us that he had given it plenty of thought and had decided that Violet was indeed the one: the one for him. He was thirty-two next month and was of an age to marry. He'd had enough of what he called "playing the field". At an opportune moment he was going to ask her to be his wife. What did we think? I am sure he knew very well that neither of us could offer an opinion as we had never met the lady.

"You must bring her with you the next time you call in, Mr Mulloy," insisted Ada. "Then we can tell you if we think you're good enough for her."

"Don't you mean if *she's* good enough for *me*?"

"No, you heard me right the first time," said Ada, with a wink in my direction.

5

At the end of the second week in March the grim cloud of war settled over the premises of Booth & Byrne for the first time. It was widely reported that a British offensive on Germany's western front had been halted. Three days of fighting around the village of Neuve Chapelle had led to a stalemate. It had been a bold plan to punch through enemy lines but the initial success was not maintained; all reports alluded to a failure of communications. The battle claimed thousands of casualties on both sides, including one of our own: my popular secretary Ethel was notified in short order that her son George was one of many men from the Manchester Regiment who were lost in the slaughter.

On behalf of the company, I visited her at her home in Salford to express our sympathies. I found a distraught woman with her stoical husband at her side; George was their only son, a twenty-two-year-old volunteer rifleman, their pride and joy. Ethel was allowed to grieve for as long as she needed to, I told her. She wanted to work, she insisted: it gave her a purpose, it would mask the pain if only for a few hours in a day. She reappeared at Cornbrook Road with a brave smile on her face in less than a week, popping her head around my office door at the first opportunity. Her hair was cut short and she was wearing a bright yellow cardigan. I had not it seen before and paid her a compliment.

"I bought it brand new yesterday, Mr Knott," she said. "For no other reason than to cheer me up."

"Are you sure you want to be at work today, Ethel?"

"It doesn't do to be sittin' at home mopin' about, Mr Knott," she said quietly. "It doesn't do at all."

Several of our staff were leaving us at that time: younger men from all divisions, wanting to volunteer to join the troops in northern France. We were not disposed to stand in their way. It was a noble cause and, in any case, business had declined and there was indisputably less to do. The docks were markedly quieter, a proportion of labourers seemed to have disappeared from the wharves, and certainly my route between home and office was less congested.

It was something of a surprise, however, when Mr South announced that he was leaving the first floor. He appeared early one morning, tapping at my door and waving my newspaper in the air. Please could he have a word in private?

He was a fine young man, twenty-five years old and as slim as a bulrush. He still had the smooth face of a boy who would struggle to grow a beard worthy of the name. Just for a minute or two, with my office door shut firmly behind him, the twinkly-eyed, jovial side of his nature, so attractive to his best friend Mr Dewsbury, was lost behind a veil of solemnity. He had decided to join up, he announced: the Lancashire Fusiliers, if they'd have him. It had been his father's regiment, he told me. He was killed during the Battle of Spion Kop in Southern Africa in the year 1900. I had heard Mr South speak of his mother from time to time but had no idea she had raised him alone from a child, no idea about the sad fate of his father.

"It will be an adventure," he added with the hint of a grin. "A chance to get out of Manchester for a bit. A chance to see something of the world."

I shook his hand and wished him the best of luck.

"Keep your head down, Mr South," I told him. "An' come back in one piece, won't you?"

I had no wiser words than that for a courageous young man who had made his decision. A warm smile before he turned to leave my room was the very least I could offer him.

Mulloy remained part of a reduced team in the accounts division and we found ourselves in conversation more and more regularly, both at work and beyond. We would often-times discuss the progress of the war, its effect on the company and on each other, and how long we thought it might last. He was of the opinion that the Germans must be beaten, even humiliated in defeat, and now that the whole grisly affair was set in motion, I was persuaded, partly by my friend, that a pacifist position had become untenable.

As promised, Ada and I were eventually introduced to Violet. She was just as beautiful as Mulloy had claimed: bright blue eyes and strawberry lips illuminated her delicate pink face, and she had her auburn hair parted and coiled loosely at the back of her head in the modern style. They visited us for tea one crisp Sunday afternoon. Ada took to her instantly and had a stream of questions about her clothes, her hair, her family, her work. Even Alfred, who generally had little time for social niceties with any friends of his parents, lingered in the room rather longer than we expected. Mulloy sat with his cup and saucer on his lap with a smile of pride on his face as the three of us bathed in the radiance of his paramour.

"I have my father to thank for my work with the railways," she told us. "He spent several years up here in administration with the LNWR. My family is from Hertfordshire. As you can probably tell."

Ada and I looked at each other. We had both heard of Hertfordshire but I doubt very much whether either of us could have placed it on a map of England. I for one had noticed that her accent was refined, as my friend had said, and to my ears neutral of regional distortions; it was some way apart from the vocal sounds I was used to hearing, not to mention from those that came out of Sidney Mulloy's own mouth.

In the following weeks we met up as a foursome again. We went for walks together, visited the amusement park across from Throstle Nest, and, on one occasion, on Ada's suggestion, played a set of tennis in Hullard Park. It was a sunny afternoon but a chilly wind blew across the court and thereby offered an excuse for misplaced shots, usually on my account, I do admit. We were still in springtime and were lucky to find the place open. One hour of scurrying around a court was enough for me: it quickly became evident that the two women were the better players, and the pair of them, on opposite sides of the net as we played mixed doubles, found it difficult to restrain their laughter (and sarcastic comments) directed at their partner's foibles with racquet and ball. In the weeks that followed, as the sun shone higher in the sky and the days grew longer, the two ladies played the game quite regularly, meeting up for a set or two of singles followed by afternoon tea whenever Violet had the occasion.

Over the long Easter weekend, which fell that year at the very start of April, most businesses and factories were closed. Time spent studying the fixture list gave Mulloy the idea that it was high time that he took me to watch a match at the United Football Ground – the place that had become such a notable addition to the dockland skyline. Easter was a good opportunity. Mulloy himself had been once before, he told me, rather more out of curiosity to visit such a stadium than due to the partisan appeal of the home team, for his favourites remained his hometown club based thirty-odd miles to the west at the mouth of the Mersey.

Professional football, along with much organised sport, was becoming an anomaly at a time when young men, the game's very constituency, were being killed or maimed in a conflict not so far away from our shores. Indeed, the Football League, the sport's ruling body, had decided at this point, no doubt under government pressure, that the 1914-15 season would be the last until the war was over. Many commentators believed that the suspension was long overdue, and even before the season ended half of the footballers had already joined the war effort and crowds were much reduced.

By Eastertime the schedule of fixtures was all but completed, but there was a run of matches over the course of the weekend including a meeting on Good Friday between Manchester United and Liverpool. Mulloy was so enthused by the prospect of watching the game that he convinced me to join him with little need for persuasion.

Neither team had enjoyed a successful season and both floundered close to the foot of the First Division league table; in fact, United were in danger of being relegated. Nevertheless, there was much pride at stake for Mulloy and we approached the stately edifice with great anticipation, joined on our eager march along the Chester Road by hundreds of other noisy fellows enjoying a Friday free from the grind of labour. These were the same streets along which the carts and waggons and bicycles and motorised vehicles bumbled past stony-faced pedestrians every morning on their way to the docks and the factories of Trafford Park. On that April afternoon, as they weaved between the trams, their faces were all the more expressive, their gait full of purpose, their voices raised in chatter that had its own cheerful musicality. Beneath a haze of tobacco smoke everyone was heading in the same direction: not to a machine or a desk or a production line, but to the brick cathedral on the horizon, the great modern stage for our city's footballers.

Inside we and ten thousand others found our places on the concrete steps that formed sloping banks of rising terraces. We had a spectacular view of the vast field with its bright white lines marked upon it, its netted goalposts at either end and the four red flags fluttering at each corner. The rooflines seemed to form the frame of a wide window offering a prospect of the high clouds floating above us all.

Even as a man with no real interest in the game, I knew of the reputation of Meredith, United's famous winger, and so I was more than curious to see him play. Mulloy had his own favourite:

"Pagnam's a better player," he insisted, as we watched the teams warming up on the pitch before the kick-off. "There he is, see, the little stocky bloke. Watch how he strikes the ball, Charlie. Sweet as a cherry."

When the game began Mulloy became less ebullient, for it was clear that the lethargic visitors in their white jerseys were no match for the more energetic, red-shirted Mancunians who ran out as winners by two goals to none. At the referee's final whistle, as we strode away from the ground, part of the high-spirited crowd, he admitted that the better team won on the day. And as a supporter of the losers, it was only proper that he should stand the first round of beers at the Red Rose public house on our way home.

6

It had been a while since I had set eyes on Daniel Harrop, who, it seemed, was reluctant to instigate any contact with me. I put it down to shyness. The fellow was not one of nature's garrulous types but I retained a soft spot for him, in part as he was one of the dwindling number of links I still had with my own Hydonian past. Whenever I thought of Danny, images of Walter Rowbotham sprang to mind: the man standing in front of our class of urchins back some forty years, or engaging in political discussion with me during a cricket match tea while I was trying to steel myself for a couple of hours of rigorous bowling. Or, in his later years, sitting by the fireside in his cottage on Jollybant Row, encouraging me to join him the next time he was to walk down to Ewen Fields to watch his beloved Hyde Football Club play a match.

With the memory of the recent visit to the United Ground fresh in my mind, and knowing that Danny too was keen on the sport, I wondered if he had ever watched the Manchester reds play. He had never mentioned it to me. Did he prefer the other local professional club, Manchester City, who, I believe, had their ground in Ardwick, not too far away? United had one remaining home fixture before the season ended, and all league football with it for the foreseeable future. The Birmingham club of Aston Villa were to be the visitors on a Monday evening at the end of April. Mulloy was sure to be interested and I resolved to invite Danny to accompany us.

One afternoon a week or so before the match, I arranged my business so that I could be in Trafford Park just as the factories were letting out at the end of the working day. The sky was a mass of darkening cloud but the rain was holding off as I stood in the jaws of a throng of men streaming out of the main gate of the Westinghouse works. I looked this way and that but there was no sign of my target. Five minutes later the exodus had thinned to ones and twos, men stopping to light a cigarette before heading home. I approached a fellow who had knelt down to tie up his bootlace.

"Do you work with a lad named Harrop?" I asked.

The man looked up at me.

"Harrop?"

"Aye. Danny Harrop. He's an engineer here."

"I know who you mean," he said, standing and rubbing his nose with the back of an oily hand. "He did work here till lately. He worked at t'other end o' t' shed."

"He *did* work here?"

"Aye, he left not so long ago. Someone said he got a better offer."

"A better offer? What does that mean, then?"

"He's at Ford's, as far as I know. I've not seen him since he left, mind. Not even comin' in from town of a mornin'."

He pulled up the collar on his jacket and made to move off.

"It's only down there, you know," he went on, pointing beyond the factory roofs and the smokestacks towards the granary building on the wharf.

I knew where he meant, of course. Ford's was the other huge factory on the park: an engineering works, American-owned, producing motor cars in large numbers. I thanked the fellow and walked on, skirting the Westinghouse site and passing other smaller works until the sprawling Ford factory loomed up ahead. Set back from the belt of wire fencing was a broad row of long work-sheds like aircraft hangars, each with its pitched roof, some with wide wooden doors gaping open: a jagged façade behind which stretched the vast spaces where, I imagined, the famous production lines were housed. At these gates too I was met with crowds of labourers coming in the opposite direction, men chatting, some laughing, others lost in their own thoughts, most smoking cigarettes. There were noisy groups of youths, clearly friends in high spirits, then older workers emerged in dribs and drabs, bodies less agile, worn down, faces lined and cracked like the grubby leather of the boots they wore.

I spotted Danny straight away, his mop of hair marking him out. He was in conversation with a man wearing a suit, then they broke apart and Danny was heading towards me alone, tightening a scarf around his neck. I called his name. He looked up and was astonished to see me outside his place of work.

"Mr Knott!"

"Charlie!"

"Charlie, aye, sorry. What are you doin' over here?"

"I was lookin' for you. What did you think? You think I'm after a Model T? I can't afford to buy a motor!"

He gave me an uncertain grin. We fell into a rhythm as we walked back together towards Throstle Nest.

"That's quite a moustache you've got there, Danny, lad!" I said.

"It were Flora's idea," he said, touching the bristles self-consciously.

"Any road," I went on, "I thought you said you were at Westie's."

"I were."

"Not no more."

"No, I got a better offer."

"Did you?"

"Well, I did have to go lookin' for it. It's a promotion, you could say. I'm actually runnin' a gang o' lads here. They call it an assembly line. It's more money. Flora's very happy about that. She's already got her mind set on rentin' a house in Pendlebury."

"Pendlebury, eh? I hear that's a nice district."

"Flora likes it out there. She's got a sister lives there."

"It'd be a longer journey into work for you."

"Suppose it would."

"I dare say there's a station, mind. Probably takes you straight to Victoria. Then at least one change, I'd say."

"Steady on, Charlie. It's only an idea she has. Nobody's sayin' we're actually movin' anywhere."

Daniel was a fast walker. Or else he was in a hurry. Before long we were approaching Throstle Nest.

"How's your team?" I asked.

"Me team? At work?"

"No, your football team."

"Alright."

"We went to watch your match at St John's, you know."

"Oh, aye?"

"Sorry we missed you."

"Oh, that game, back end o' last year. Aye, I were crocked, if I remember right. I got clattered the week before. This here ankle. Swollen up like a pumpkin, it were. I couldn't play for a month or so. I didn't start playin' again, really, till about February time."

The lights of Old Trafford railway station were coming into view.

"You catchin' the train home tonight or walkin' it?" I asked.

"Train. It looks like rain."

"Well, then, Danny, here's an idea for you before we go our separate ways. Do you fancy an evenin' at the football? United at home a week on Monday?"

While he hesitated, as I guessed he would, I told him about Mulloy, about the match against Liverpool, and that the next one would probably be the last until the war was over.

"I did wonder why you'd come out o' your way to find me. Monday week, you say? Aye, go on. I've not been since the season before last. Go on, I'll come with you. Mind you, they're not worth watchin', really, are they?"

Another ambiguous grin.

We barely had time to make arrangements to meet at Isabella Street on the twenty-seventh before a heavy shower beat down on the scene and we scampered off in our separate ways for shelter.

Daniel Harrop had never set foot in my house before. There was a little time between the end of his shift and the kick-off, so I had invited him to spend half an hour of leisure around our kitchen table before we set off for the football ground. We shared a pot of tea, a thick slice of Ada's fruit cake and a wedge of Cheshire cheese, which I knew he would appreciate.

My wife sat with us as we ate.

"Are you cold, Danny?" she asked suddenly.

The man had a mouth full of cheese and could do no more than shake his head.

"It's just that you've kept your gloves on inside."

I too had noticed this but had let it pass. Ada was not so reticent.

"Yes, I have." he said upon swallowing.

"Isn't it awkward lifting that cup with them on?"

They were loose-fitting, thick gloves made of grey wool.

"Suppose so," he said, studying the garments as though he had never noticed them covering his hands until that moment. "A bit."

"Keep them on if you wish," insisted Ada, leaving him no option other than to reluctantly pull them off, while we watched.

"They were Walter's, you know," he said, addressing me. "The last gift me mother bought for him before she passed."

Immediately we all could see his right hand was roughly wrapped in a discoloured bandage.

"Oh, my goodness!" exclaimed Ada. "What have you done, you poor man?"

Danny coughed, swallowed and looked down at his hand.

"It's nowt. Dunna worry."

But Ada was already hovering, making to touch the bandage.

"Let me repair that for you. It's falling off, anyway. Is there a wound beneath it?"

I saw that Danny was loath to engage but he had no choice.

"It's a burn," he said.

"A burn or a scald?"

"A burn. I got too close to a candle. Daft, I know."

"Right, stand up, Danny. Let's get you cleaned up."

Within five minutes Ada had removed the old bandage, washed the poor man's palm, applied an antiseptic ointment to an area of festering rawness and tidily covered his hand with a fresh strip of gauze.

At that moment Alfred appeared in the kitchen, looking puzzled to see his mother rearranging the contents of her medical box. He watched as Danny pulled on his gloves again, and hesitated to shake his damaged hand. Danny smiled sheepishly and offered the boy his left. I could not remember whether the two had previously met. I announced their names just to be sure, but Alfred had already helped himself to a slice of cake and with his mouth half-full he looked directly at me and, to my surprise, declared that he wanted to come to the match with us. Without looking I could tell that Ada was smiling. I had more than an inkling that she had encouraged this opportunity for a moment of bonding between father and son.

So, it was the three of us who met Mulloy at the corner of Warwick Road as it crossed the main Chester Road. He was watching out for us, with his hands in his coat pockets. Crowds of men were drifting past, fewer in number than on

Good Friday – popular enthusiasm for the season's football was already a long way past its zenith. We exchanged greetings, I quickly introduced Danny to Mulloy, and we set off in step towards the ground. Alfred liked Mulloy, this much I did know. There was a minute when I was separated from the three of them by a passing bicyclist and I observed them from behind: my son was listening intently to some joke Mulloy was telling, while on the Liverpudlian's right Danny too was laughing loud and freely. From left to right and roughly ten years between each of them, I was seeing some vague incarnation of the unknowable future, then the present, fair of face and slick of hair, and finally the past, wearing a pair of an old man's gloves. Then another thought occurred to me: a barely remembered notion from a Shakespearean monologue about the seven ages of man, from infancy to a time of second childishness. Here I saw three of those stages sharing a humorous tale and, I supposed, myself a few paces behind them at a later stage, that of *the lean and slippered pantaloon*.

Mulloy had pulled a small paper bag out of a pocket and was offering its contents to his new comrades.

"Sorry, Charlie," he said as I caught up with them, to find him screwing up the empty paper. "I only had three bits of toffee brittle left."

Danny and Alfred were giggling like schoolboys, their mouths full of toffee, as I joined their ranks a few seconds too late for a share of the confectionery.

The stadium, so grand and designed for so many, was echoey and inappropriate, I thought, for a small crowd, and the players too seemed to be less than completely engaged that evening. There was an uneasy atmosphere about the place, reflecting the incongruity of so many athletic young men exerting themselves for sport at a time when the country was at war. Nevertheless, we all enjoyed the contest, the skills on display, and a home victory by one goal to nil.

At the end the ground slowly emptied of its spectators, their conversations dwindled into mumblings, their footsteps heavy on the shadowy roads, their faces set solemnly against the darkening sky. We were walking away from something, all of us, wrapped in our own thoughts, walking away from an ending, from a closing. And each with eyes fixed on our own path towards the dusky streets of the city, we were striding together towards a new something, the next something, towards a future for each one of us that nobody could really ever imagine.

Part Four
1916

1

There were plenty of members of the labouring classes in our corner of England who were familiar with the dangers of the noxious chemicals that were part and parcel of their everyday experiences of working in the textile industry. From the pressurised steaming that was introduced in poorly ventilated weaving sheds to make the cotton yarn more tractable, to the contaminates in the dusty air inhaled by the spinners and the scutchers of the carding rooms. Thence to the bleaching and dyeing processes where exposure to the fumes of harsh chemicals such as the dioxides of sulphur and nitrogen presented a dreadful array of threats to workers: to their lungs, their eyes, their throats. Disease and infirmity came slowly, oftentimes invisibly, over a period of years.

Nothing they had heard from consumptive grandparents, however, could have prepared the generation of young men who, while suffering in the grim battlefields of northern France, were now being exposed to a new danger: exploding canisters of poisonous gas fired above their heads by the Germans.

From the comfort of my office I felt as helpless and outraged as everyone else I met. As a form of weapon, the use of chlorine gas and sulphurous variants was explicitly illegal under a series of conventions. Nevertheless, I found myself reading regular newspaper reports of incidents in which Allied troops were suffering from gas attacks that would irritate the lungs and cause choking within short order. Principally used as a defensive tactic, by the third year of the stalemate the Germans had developed a more corrosive, so-called mustard gas: soldiers gave accounts of a dusky yellow cloud, of men's lungs blistering, their eyes stinging, their capacity to breathe reduced within seconds. Protection from the effects was pitiful: troops were given damp linen masks (sometimes soaked in bicarbonate of soda) to tie over their faces, or for the luckier ones there was the more sophisticated measure of a pad of lint and a length of elasticated tape. Thousands of men were poisoned, many fatally. Later in the year it was both depressing and inevitable that the British army should be fighting fire with fire: our own laboratories provided the science for factories to manufacture gas bombs that were to be aimed at the enemy for as long as the conflict dragged on.

News of the war was relentlessly grim at that time. The Allies' attempt to control access to the Black Sea, what became known as the Gallipoli campaign, had ended in disaster. There had been more successful campaigns in Africa but victories had come at a heavy price. Meanwhile the trench warfare on the Germans' western front edged this way and that with terrible losses on both sides for little gain. Reading between the lines of the official reports of battles and skirmishes, it was not difficult to sense that morale among the troops was low, especially during the cruel months of winter.

To few observers' surprise but many people's dismay, the British Government passed a Military Service Act in January 1916. More than dismay to the families of single men aged between eighteen and forty-one, to parents like Ada and myself: it was with dread that we read that conscription was to be introduced with only two months' notice. There were exemptions, of course, for certain professions and the medically unfit, but into no such category did our son Alfred fall. He would be released by the *Courier* without question, and the theatre would let him go – the former was a faltering concern and he was not strictly a paid employee of the latter when all was said and done.

The boy himself was stoical; he resigned himself to the fact of the matter with a good grace that both surprised and impressed me. I had no doubt that he had his darker moments in private: Alfred saw himself as a writer, a lyricist, a gentle, creative young man. How would he be, holding a rifle, never mind firing one? How would he be, sheltering in the squalor of a trench, risking his life each time an officer sent him on an errand, or, even worse, out and over the top?

"You might be cynical about the politicians making decisions, Father," he said to me the day the letter from the War Office arrived. "But I believe they are doing it for the right reasons."

We were in the kitchen, drinking tea. I kept quiet, numbed by the prospect of my only child in a military uniform being shot at in a foreign field.

"I'm a patriot," he went on, "and the Germans must be defeated."

"I'm a patriot too," I said, wanting to add that I believed England could do better than this, better than to be run by a class of men who so rarely got their hands dirty, never mind getting their tunics covered in blood. I did not say these things. I knew the moment was wrong, but there would come a time when this war was over. Alfred had heard me voice my reservations a dozen times before in any case.

He approached me, brushed away his fringe with his fingers and fixed me with his pale blue eyes.

"Don't worry, Father," he said, "I'll be back before you know it. I'll look after myself. I'll be a survivor, you can bank on it."

I smiled, pulled him into a trembling embrace, smelled the sweet oil on his hair. For an instant I believed him. I believed in his invincibility.

The piano music coming from the sitting room stopped. As he pulled away from me, his mother appeared at the door, her hair loosened and fallen to her shoulders. She too had read the message and baulked at the prospect but I had yet to see her cry. The piece she had been playing was a jolly air, a release, I suppose, something to raise her spirit.

"Alfred," she said, arms open in invitation. "Come and play something with me. Something gay."

I knew he had what he might have considered better things to do, but he was his mother's son and could refuse her nothing.

"Something life-affirming," he added with a smile, taking her hand and stepping out of the kitchen at her side.

I watched them disappear, found myself a chair to sit on and waited for the first tentative notes. Presently Ada started and then stopped. Then I heard her start again: the rhythm of a slow waltz, which Alfred would join and together they would accelerate into a joyful swirl of music. I wanted to smile, to let the dancing notes take me away from myself but I could not quite allow them.

His empty teacup sat on the table in front of me. He had several days with us before he was required to enlist. Every passing hour the sands of time would be as precious as grains of gold dust.

2

Early one Monday morning I bumped into Mulloy on the stairs. On the draughty and poorly-lit first-floor landing, to be precise. As I arrived on the way up, he was descending from the second floor, clutching his black leather briefcase.

"Mornin', Mull," I said. "Is Mr Pollitt up there? I was hopin' to catch him for a word today."

"He was," the accountant replied, pausing to straighten the knot on his necktie with his free hand. "You've just missed him. I'm surprised you didn't cross him on your way up."

"Never mind. I'll telephone him later on."

"Can *we* have a word, Charlie? When you've got five minutes."

"Course we can, What's to do? Is it business?"

"No, it's not business, as it happens. It's personal stuff."

"Well, I didn't think it'd be business, to be honest. There's not so much goin' on at the moment, is there?"

It was a fact that blockades in many European ports, the constant threat of German submarines (so-called U-boats) in the North Atlantic and the restrictions on trade across the globe had begun to affect shipping more and more seriously with each passing month. Neither ships registered with neutral countries nor commercial ocean liners were spared attack if the Germans suspected them of carrying ammunition. This was the case in the controversial incident the previous summer when *Lusitania*, a great Cunard passenger ship that had *not* been commissioned by the Royal Navy, was torpedoed close to Ireland. It had sailed from New York and over one hundred of those lost were Americans.

The empty berths in our docks were noticeable, while certain ships were lingering longer than usual for spurious repairs rather than risking the high seas. Many commercial sailors had been drafted to help their navies in the war at sea, and trade to and from continental Europe had all but stopped. New contracts were drawn up with shipping companies from neutral countries such as Norway and Sweden who could partly fill the void by preserving the fragile links between Britain and the Americas. It was not unusual at that time to see groups of broad-shouldered sailors with short blond hair strolling around the streets of Manchester. Nor to hear one or two enquiring of a shopkeeper, in broken English, which was the easiest way back to the docks.

On many of these operational matters I did indeed need to confer with Mr Pollitt and, on occasion, with Mr Byrne himself.

I glanced at my pocket watch.

"How about now?" I said. "I'll ask Ethel to make us a pot o'tea."

"Perfect."

Of all the office staff beyond my door, only the ever-punctual Mr Dewsbury and his new protégé, a sixteen-year-old we called Master Crompton, had reported for work so far, along with Ethel and another stenographer, a little mouse of a girl whose name I could never remember. Annie? Aimee? With the heavy door closed, my room guaranteed a satisfactory level of privacy. Nevertheless, I had pulled the armchairs closer together and, ten minutes later, with an empty teapot and crockery on the table at our knees, we sat smoking cigarettes, complaining about the weather, sugar shortages and the high price of fish.

"How's Alfred?" Mulloy asked.

"Putting on a brave face," I answered. "He went to say his goodbyes to his grandparents yesterday."

My friend nodded thoughtfully.

When Alfred was a child, he considered himself deprived to have only one set of grandparents. He told me so several times, not so much blaming me for the fact, but wondering aloud how my parents figured in his own story. He knew something about my mother Elizabeth, a weaver who had worked in several of the mills in Hyde, and I related what I knew about my father Ralph, the navvy who had been killed in an accident while laying railway tracks in the Pennines. That I could remember no more than that was a source of frustration for both of us.

"An' what about you, Mull? What's on your mind?"

We had talked about conscription only briefly, the pair of us. Of course, it was a matter that affected us all: our workforce at Booth & Byrne would be somewhat reduced, and there was talk of inviting Mr Horridge back to cover for absentees, provided he was kept away from the telephone. Mulloy himself was of an age to enlist but so far he had seemed reluctant to accept the fact. Only now, loosening his tie, edging forward on his seat, his handsome face a little pale and drawn, was he prepared to share his anxiety.

"They've been in touch, Charlie," he said, stubbing out his cigarette. "You know, the War Office. They've given me a date."

I nodded, let him talk.

"I've got a bit more than a month." He swallowed. "But that's alright. It's plenty of time. Plenty of time. Provided she says yes."

He looked up and caught my puzzled expression.

"Violet. I'm goin' to marry her. Skip the engagement, just marry her. Man an' wife. Me an' Violet. I told you she's the one, Charlie. You do like her, don't you?"

This had come straight out of the blue but it made perfect sense: married men were exempt from the demands of the War Office.

"Yes," I said. "I like her. We both of us do."

He was smiling to himself, vindicated.

"Ada's very fond o' Violet," I added. "But surely you don't need our blessin'. You know in your own heart, surely, if you want her to be your wife?"

"You're right, Charlie. Quite right. Wise words, as always." He patted me on the knee. "Wise words. Well, I've made my mind up. I'm gonna ask her tonight. An' if she says yes, then we'll make our plans right away."

He stood up, retrieved his briefcase, and faced me again.

"Do you think I'm a coward, Charlie?" he asked, running his fingers through his hair. It was a simple enough question but one with an edge to it.

"No. No, I think not."

"Your son is a better man, though. A better man than me. You think that, don't you?"

I had to pause. It was not a comparison I had ever contemplated.

"Alfred's circumstances are different," I said finally. "If he were engaged, if he had a girl, then I'd hope he might do just as you're doin'. But he's not engaged, is he? He's not got himself a girl yet. He's just a twenty-year-old lad, a youth with no

101

strings attached. He's got no choice, has he? Bein' a coward's not an option. No, you're not a coward, Mull, you're just followin' your instincts, and I for one wouldn't judge you for one minute."

"Thanks for the tea," he said, edging towards the door.

I stood up and watched him leave.

"It'll all be for nothin'," he said, turning back to me with a rueful smile on his lips. "They'll probably extend the orders to include married men if the war really does go to shit like it looks like it's goin' to."

3

12th April 1916

Dear Mother, Dear Father,

I hope this finds you both well. I'm writing to let you know that I am doing well at our training camp. There's no need to worry about me.

I can't say where we are exactly. Neither will I be allowed to mention locations when we get over to France. For now, we are in some part of Shropshire, I think. There are hills and woods and river valleys and farmhouses nearby. We were told the land around the front line would be quite similar. It's quite a beautiful place, to be honest, and the weather has been grand. They've given us shorts to wear and my legs are getting brown already.

There are up to two hundred lads here, I reckon, always on the move. New groups arriving and others leaving every few days. They're from all over, not just Manchester. There are Scots amongst them who we can't understand when they talk. There are sixteen of us in our hut. The beds aren't so comfortable – just a straw mattress on planks – but no-one's complaining. The food's not so bad. We have a lot of bread and jam, some stew, soup, plenty of tea. I'm missing Mother's cooking already! Yesterday they gave us our jabs. For typhoid, the nurse said.

Last night we went out on a night exercise. We were driven into the forest at midnight, split up and then given maps. We had to find a treasure before daylight. I enjoyed it, as we had some clever lads in our team and we found it no trouble. It was a wooden box in a churchyard with six bottles of beer inside. We do a lot of marching – they call it square-bashing – and physical exercise too. Some lads are useless – two left feet! And we do drills and target practice with rifles on a range. I'm not bad. You'd be proud of me, Father. They like a singalong in our hut. There's a pair of brothers from Stockport who do a nice harmony.

So, just to say, don't be worrying about me. I'm busy and I'm prepared to do my bit for the King. We've got a few more weeks here yet, so they say, but I will be leaving England sometime next month, I suppose.

With lots of love,

Alfred (also known as Private Knott!)

I was already starting to avert my eyes from newspaper reports of the war. I had an impression of what Alfred was going to find in France and I was reluctant to have it presented in sharper focus. There were other stories in the pages, of course; other currents stirring beyond the battlefields, and two names repeatedly caught my eye at that time.

The first was Patrick Pearse, a poet, a barrister, an Irish republican who hated the British. Irish Home Rule, a contentious issue for generations, had been passed in principle by Parliament in 1914, but was paused when the war began. As thousands of Irish soldiers loyal to Britain enlisted, there remained many who would not. Meanwhile two opposing groups, those who still opposed Home Rule and those who wanted a complete split from Britain, had begun to arm themselves clandestinely in advance of the violence to come. Needless to say, the alignments were sectarian in nature.

Pearse was a member of the latter group, dedicated to the overthrow of British Protestant rule in Ireland.

The second was a Russian, a political activist named Vladimir Lenin. He was a disciple of Karl Marx, whose writings of his time in Manchester had moved me greatly in my younger days, and his socialist views were anathema to the Russian monarchy. Among others of similar persuasion, Lenin was in exile in Switzerland, observing the effects of the war on Germany's eastern front. It appeared that poor morale amongst the Russian soldiers and antipathy towards the government of the Tsar were becoming factors in calls for a change in that distant country.

The departure of our son was but a small, personal element in the greater moment. The world was already changing but it seemed to me that until now we had seen only a fraction of the upheaval yet to come.

Mulloy and Violet disappeared for over a fortnight. He must have been granted dispensation from Osmund Pollitt but his absence was not discussed between us. I had no idea what arrangements were made at the telephone switchboard of London Road railway station. Violet had accepted my friend's proposal, it was clear, and, we assumed, with great joy. Ada was a little put out that she was unable to play a small part in helping her choose a wedding dress, for example, and apparently Dooley's of Cross Street did a delightful line in accessories on which she would have liked to offer advice.

The couple were not to be seen until they reappeared without warning just as casually as if they had been on a day-trip to the seaside. Mulloy turned up at Booth & Byrne one day with a smile on his face and a wedding certificate in his jacket pocket. He produced it unexpectedly, waving it in front of my eyes like the winning ticket in a tombola. They had got married in Hertfordshire, he reported. A lovely little village church. Violet's family had made all the arrangements. It was a quiet affair.

"You know, nice an' private," he said, tucking the certificate back inside his pocket. "Close family only. Anyway, it's done, Charlie. We're together, a proper married couple, an' we can get on with our lives now, can't we?"

4

Once his unit's military training was summarily completed – rudimentary by necessity – Alfred was posted abroad without being given the chance to come home one final time. So our farewells at the end of March had been the last occasion we had to embrace him and tell him how we loved him so. Ada had held back her tears until he had left us, striding away in a uniform that for all his pride in it did not really suit him, as we all knew deep down. It was like kitting out a surgeon for a shift down a coal mine.

As he departed, bound for the cruel lottery of the battle-field, we were reminded in a most brutal manner that bullets and bombs were part of a landscape that existed not only on the European continent but also on the British island to our west.

Of all the problems facing our government, the constitutional future of Ireland was the knottiest, brutally crossing lines of empire, of nationhood and of religion. It was something that I can remember discussing with Walter Row-botham when the notion of Home Rule was first supported by Mr Gladstone thirty years earlier. As both Protestant Unionists and Catholic Nationalists had formed shadowy paramilitary groups in 1913, the prospect of civil strife was averted only by the war with Germany. Many nationalists fought for the British cause, but there were others who saw the war as an opportunity to strike, even engaging German support in the process.

I recall reading the newspaper report of the events in Dublin on Easter Monday: bands of rebels, the so-called army of the Irish Republic, over one thousand strong and armed with pistols and rifles, took hold of strategic buildings in the centre of the city. The British army, taken by surprise, struggled to emerge from their barracks. Patrick Pearse, revelling in the name Pádraic, standing defiantly outside the General Post Office, read aloud the proclamation of the Republic.

In the days that followed, reinforcements, fresh artillery supplies and a gunboat in the harbour gradually gave the British the upper hand; at the end of six days of street fighting, the Irish surrendered. Martial law was imposed, which did nothing to quell anti-British sentiment. Nor, at the beginning of May, did the execution by firing squad of sixteen of the most prominent rebels, including Pearse. Almost five hundred people were killed in the Rising, mostly civilians, and the centre of Dublin was horribly damaged. It was a tragic event concurrent with an avalanche of tragic events and, to my mind, did nothing to advance the prospect of a peaceful solution to the politics of the island.

One evening not so very long after what she called "the emergency wedding", Ada had a brusque question for me the moment I walked into the house. She must have been dwelling on it for most of the afternoon. Looking back on it, I wish she had saved the question for another time, certainly another day, as I had been working hard on shipping contracts – finessing details of new ones, cancelling some, amending others – and my head was still full of caveats and conditions and compensation clauses. Of course, I did hear her question. My answer was slow arrive, however, as I failed to grasp straight away exactly what she was driving at.

"Charlie, do you believe everything about Violet?"

I was in the process of untying my shoelaces, ready to take the weight of my feet, thinking about lighting up a cigarette.

"I beg your pardon?"

She repeated the question, standing over me like a kindly schoolmistress.

"Everythin' about Violet?" I echoed. "Ada, love, what do you mean?"

She took the armchair next to the one I had slumped into, flattened her dress over her knees, and leaned forward to place a hand on one of mine.

"I'm having my doubts," she said, looking into my eyes for a reaction.

"Doubts? I thought she were a friend o' yours."

"Oh, she is."

"Games o' tennis, shoppin' together, teas in town…"

"I know. You're right. We've got quite close, in spite of the difference in age."

"She treats you like an older sister."

"I suppose she does."

"An' to you, she's like a younger sister. The sister you once said you wished you'd had."

"You're right. You're quite right."

"But …"

"Yes, there is a but, Charlie. Actually, there's more than one. It's since they got married. Have you noticed any difference in Mull?"

"No. No, I can't say I have. With so many men missin', we're all busy at work, mind. I've not had much chance to talk to him, you know, as a friend."

Ada sat back in her chair, took a deep breath. I fidgeted with my cigarette case and decided I didn't want to smoke after all.

"So, what's she done, your Violet, any road?" I asked.

Ada sat up again, clasping her hands together on her lap.

"We were talking about their wedding day. Just yesterday, this was, while we were out at Parker's having lunch. You know, she has Wednesdays off. I was asking all sorts of questions. You know what I'm like, Charlie." She smiled.

"Nosey."

"Not nosey. I'm inquisitive. I'm curious. Interested. For instance, I asked about her bridesmaids and Mull's best man. Why he didn't have one. That's what he told you, isn't it? He didn't have one?"

"That's what he said. It were all too much of a hurry."

"Well, Violet said her brother was his best man."

"Her brother? Not his brother?"

"Her brother. Violet's brother. Well, whoever it was, he couldn't easily have forgotten, could he? Not at his own wedding, just a few weeks ago."

"I don't think's it's that important, Ada, love."

"Well, one of them's wrong. And another thing. At the café. We had a waitress serving us, Alice, I think she's called. She's served us before, even learned our names. A polite girl, she is, and quite the suffragette. I've seen her at meetings a time or two. Anyway, Alice, courteous as ever, asks her if she's ready to order, calls her Miss Clark, as she would. *Are you ready to order, Miss Clark?* Alice doesn't know her married name, does she? Doesn't even know she's married at all. Violet answers her without a second thought. No *You can call me Mrs Mulloy now.* No thought of showing Alice her wedding ring. No smile of pride."

"It's too soon, I suppose."

"Too soon?"

"She's not got used to bein' Mrs Mulloy."

"Hm."

"What are you sayin', Ada? Do you not believe they were married?"

She hesitated a moment, picking at a thumbnail with her teeth.

"I don't know. Maybe I am jumping to conclusions. Everything being in such a rush. And in Hertfordshire. Hertfordshire? It's a convenient place where nobody can trace them. Nobody we know can vouch for them. I asked her if she had any wedding photographs to show me."

"What did she say?"

"She hadn't any with her. Some were taken but her mother was having them put into an album."

"Is that mutton I can smell?" I said, ready to let the subject drop. My wife had more to say, however.

"The other thing I thought was odd was the last time she came round here."

"There's summat else? You're becomin' quite the detective!"

"It was just about a week ago. I left her in the sitting room while I fetched some fruit loaf. We'd been talking about a trip to the seaside together, you know, when the weather gets a bit better. The four of us: you and Mull too. Anyway, as I came back in from the kitchen to ask her if she wanted a little butter on the side, I found her up by the piano reading through a couple of suffragette magazines."

"Is that a crime?"

"I said nothing, but I am sure I'd not left them out on top of the piano like that. I'm sure they were in my attaché case. I'd not had them out for weeks. The case was still by the window seat where I'd left it, but she must have been rooting inside it. She must have been, Charlie. And she's shown no interest in those magazines before."

"She knows where your sympathies lie?"

"Oh, of course, she does. We've talked about all that, but she never really showed much interest. She says she's not political. She's never been encouraged to be. I told her that's because men don't want her to be. She's too obedient, too submissive. We have a little grumble about it together sometimes. You know, a grumble about men and their arrogant ways."

Ada paused for breath. I smiled, mainly to myself.

"Anyway," she went on, "there she is, surreptitiously studying my magazines that she's taken – without permission – from my attaché case."

"Did you say owt?"

"No. I just asked her about the butter. When I came back Violet was keen to talk about the seaside again. No, I left it. I wanted time to think about it, I suppose."

I pulled myself out of the chair, loosened my collar and undid my necktie.

"I'm goin' for a wash," I announced.

"And then she was asking about Dowson," said Ada, before I had taken more than three paces.

"Dowson?"

"Henry Dowson. That reverend friend of yours."

"He's not really a friend o' mine."

"Well, you know him. He lives in Hyde, doesn't he? Didn't he write to you when Walter was ill?"

I had forgotten the letter, but Ada was right. Dowson *had* written to me. I still had the letter somewhere.

"What did she ask?"

"Just if you knew him. How well you knew him. Were you in regular correspondence?"

"Why would she want to know?"

"She said she had a distant relative who was buried in the chapel yard. Hyde Chapel, that's the place, isn't it?"

I nodded.

"Someone related to her mother. There was some query over the plot."

"I thought they were all from Hertfordshire?"

"Well, that's what she said. You see what I mean, Charlie? It's getting to the stage where I'm beginning to think that she's not completely believable."

I needed a little time to think. If Ada had her doubts then there had to be some substance to them. She disappeared into the kitchen to give the stew a stir.

Over our meal I returned to the subject.

"Do you think Violet might be workin' for the government?" I asked, nudging my empty plate to one side.

"What do you mean? For the police force?"

"I don't know exactly. Summat like that. We are at war, aren't we? There's a lot o' paranoia about. Anti-war sentiment might be looked on as subversive. You know, unpatriotic."

"Well, exactly," she said, fixing her eyes on mine. "Need I look any further than across this table?"

"I've changed my mind on that score, Ada, as well you know. I've no time for the politicians, but I'm not anti-British, am I?"

"No, of course you're not. But neither of us is exactly pro-establishment."

I was finding it hard to understand where all of this was heading. Ada was still talking:

"Maybe that's why she's interested in us. Why she befriended us. Didn't you once say that that man Dowson had German sympathies?"

"I don't know about sympathies. He loves the country. I know that for a fact. I think he was educated there. He speaks the language, Walter did tell me once. One of his daughters spent time in Dresden, I remember."

"Isn't he a non-conformist? Some kind of socialist?"

"He's a non-conformist minister, yes, he is, but that's not illegal. It's not even subversive."

Ada too had finished her meal. Placing her cutlery neatly across her plate, she sat back in her chair and dabbed her mouth with a napkin.

"She works in the telephone exchange, doesn't she?"

"Violet? You know very well she does. At London Road."

"She says she does."

114

"Yes, she says she does. She's said it a dozen times."

"It fits together, doesn't it?"

"What does?"

"Listening in to people's telephone conversations. Poking about in people's bags. Asking too many questions. Lying about being married."

"Slow down, Ada. You're jumpin' to conclusions, here."

"She's a spy, Charlie. The woman is a government spy, believe you me."

"So what does that make Mull, then? He introduced her to us, din't he?"

"He's either an innocent stooge – is that the word? – or he's an accomplice."

"An accomplice? So Mull's a spy an' all? Now you *are* being paranoid."

"Maybe I am. Maybe I'm not. Maybe I have very good reason to be."

I had known Sidney Mulloy for over a year and had nothing but admiration for him. He was a valued colleague and had become a reliable and entertaining friend.

"Do you talk about politics much?" my wife was asking. "The two of you? The war? The government?"

"He knows how I feel about the war, about the government. He agrees with me. He calls himself a patriot, as I do, but he's got no time for Asquith. His father was a docker, an' a union man till he became an invalid – he took an army bullet in the Liverpool strike back in 1911."

This information was new to Ada, and yet as disturbing as it was, she refused to be knocked off her course.

"How do you know all of that is true?" she asked.

"'Cause he told me, Ada. 'Cause I believed him."

"He could have been lying."

"Why would he make it up?"

"Because that's what they do. Spies. *Agents provocateurs.* That's what they do. They pretend. They act a part. They deceive."

I drew a deep breath. Then another.

"Let me deal with Mull," I said. "I'm sure he's as true as an arrow."

"And Violet?"

"I'm still to be convinced. You an' those Pankhurst women see threats in every shadow. But we'll set her a trap."

"A trap?"

"Aye, to see how inquisitive she really is. Is she just curious or is she actually hunting for evidence that'll damn us both as traitors? In her mind, at least."

It struck me that for someone who was determined to cast aspersions as to our allegiance (or otherwise) to the establishment's interpretation of patriotism, there were three avenues they could pursue:

Firstly, Ada was a well-known member of the sisterhood, at least in Manchester, both as a suffragist and lately more sympathetic to the suffragettes too. She had broken no laws, had spent no time in prison, but there was literature pertaining to women's rights in every cupboard and drawer in the house.

As for me, anybody who knew me would describe me as a radical thinker (assuredly a thinker, or even a talker, much more than an activist), a believer in a more equitable society, a holder of so-called left-wing opinions. Socialist Party pamphlets and old copies of *The Daily Citizen* were to be found in my study, along with books on Marx and Engels, not to mention various articles I had kept about Lenin and his followers in Russia.

It was the third avenue, the least convincing of all in fact, which angered me the most. I had no sympathies for the Germans, certainly not the Kaiser and his generals, not even for his people. I cannot remember ever meeting one on whom to form an opinion. But if Violet Mulloy, née Clark, was intent on linking me somehow with the Reverend Henry Dowson – who himself was no traitor, I was convinced – then I wanted to be sure that that indeed was an angle of her investigation.

The next time the woman called at Isabella Street, Ada was to invite her to my study, ostensibly to show her the map I had framed on the wall above my desk: a most impressive print of the original plan of the route of the Ship Canal. Visible on the desk, on top of a pile of other correspondence, would be the letter from the Reverend Dowson – the only one I had ever received from the man – informing me of the illness of our mutual friend Rowbotham and signed off *Grüss Gott. Grüss Gott*, indeed. Would those words quicken the blood in her veins?

The letter was still in its envelope, which I labelled "Dowson" in heavy pencil by the postage stamp. I removed the page and between its fold I placed a fine hair from my head before returning it to its envelope. I left the article lying at a random (yet deliberate) angle in relation to the stack beneath it; any movement would be recognisable after the event. And there was no justifiable reason to move it at all beyond an urge to snoop. Ada would leave the room for a moment under a pretext, allowing Violet the opportunity to pry if that indeed was her compulsion.

On the arranged date, I returned home earlier than usual, walking through a rain shower rather than waiting for the dark clouds to pass over, so eager was I to discover the outcome. Without even removing my dripping coat, I headed directly to the study. I could smell Violet's perfume in the room. The light was fading but I needed no illumination to discern instantly that the envelope was not exactly on the spot where I had left it. The standard lamp at my back suddenly lit up the space and I heard Ada's voice behind me.

"She read it, didn't she?"

I placed my spectacles on the bridge of my nose, pulled out the letter, carefully unfolded it and found no hair resting in its crease.

"She did, my dear," I said quietly, turning to face her. "It looks like you were right about Violet after all."

I was intrigued to see how Mulloy had adapted to having to share the small flat he had in Ordsall with a new wife.

The evenings were getting lighter, the air a little warmer and workers were in less of a mind to scurry home at the end of a day's shift to a plate of hot food and the family hearth. One afternoon I went down into the accounts division and found him with his shirt sleeves rolled up above his elbows, surrounded by page after page of figures, with the fingers of his right hand resting on the keys of an adding machine. A cigarette was burning out in an ashtray littered with butts.

"Who'd want to do my job?" he laughed.

"It's better than bein' down a coal pit," I said.

"Suppose it is."

"Or holdin' a rifle in a trench on the front line."

"Hm."

"Any road, Mull, when you've done for today, how about we go to th'Albert for a pint?"

The Prince Albert was a public house in Ordsall where we had drunk together once before. There was a yard where they put out tables in the better weather and it made for a good place to sit and talk. It was a stone's throw from the building Mulloy lived in, and there was a good chance we would call in at his flat at some point. Especially if I made such a suggestion.

"Aye, I'll be ready for a beer," he said, taking his eyes off the sheets of paper and raising them to meet mine.

"Happen Violet'll want to join us."

"Violet? She'll be at work."

"She'll be back home by six, won't she?"

Mulloy turned his attention back to his lists of names and numbers.

"Won't she?" I asked.

"Violet's still livin' in town," he said, stubbing out what remained of his cigarette.

"She's not moved in yet? Whyever not? Man an' wife livin' apart? You're not sharin' the matrimonial home?"

"She's staying up in town till her contract runs out. Makes sense. An' she reckons it's more comfortable than my place."

"I see."

"Then we'll be lookin' for somethin' bigger."

"So you're still livin' on your own."

"For the time bein'."

"That's a bit sad, I think, if you don't mind me sayin'."

"Say what you like, Charlie."

"It sounds like a marriage o' convenience to me."

"Why do you say that?" he snapped – a spikier response than I had expected to a remark meant as a joke.

"Sorry, Mull, I meant nowt by it."

He gave me a testy stare.

"But you'll come for a pint," I said. "When you've done?"

He turned away to concentrate on his task.

"I'll see how I get on with this lot."

I patted him on the shoulder and left him alone. Colleagues, some of whom had no doubt been straining to hear our conversation, were dutifully engrossed in their ledgers. One or two looked up as I passed them, nodding in acknowledgment.

"I might have to work late," Mulloy shouted to me as I reached the door.

When I called into his division on my way out of the offices two or three hours later, his chair was empty, his desk had been tidied and there was no sign of the fellow. One of the clerks looked across to tell me that Mr Mulloy had left half an hour ago without a word of goodbye to anyone.

5

Dearest Mother and Father,

I hope you are well. My life has changed a lot in these past weeks. I am writing from the support line where it's not so bad. They move us up and down the lines. The forward trenches are the worst, of course. Closer to the Germans and their shelling. And you're the first ones up the ladders and over the top if there's an operation been ordered. I've done that a few times already – out into what they call no-man's land – mending wires, scavenging, out with the waggon picking up wounded men. Even scouting at night. It's a mess out there and no mistake. The land is churned up like a great bog.

It's warm here and we've not had any rain this week, which is a blessing. Here and further back in the reserve trenches we get regular food. Usually corned beef in a stew and jam and bread. There's always plenty of cigarettes. We get a bit of cheese now and again. Proper Cheshire it is and all. Not too stale. Of course it reminds me of home and Mother's lovely recipe with baked cauliflower.

Our unit is due one more spell at the front and then we should have some leave. That means a base in a town like Amien or Abbeyville. I'm not sure if I'm spelling them right. I've been looking at the maps when I get the chance. If this letter is censored by the sergeant you'll know why!

That's all for now. We have to move.

God bless,

Alfred

Late one evening I found myself walking home southwards through the dark streets of the Ordsall district of Salford. A half-moon was veiled by thin, high clouds shifting in bands across the deep blue sky.

I had been invited to supper with Jeremiah Shawcross, an old friend who still lived in the house on Regent Road where he had been born some fifty years earlier. Long resigned to life as a bachelor, he shared the modest accommodation with his mother who, though now quite elderly, was in respectable health and more than capable of cooking a wholesome meal for the three of us.

I had first met Shawcross in my early days in Manchester; being youthful and athletic, he was used as a messenger, a runner as it were, between various foremen managing operations on the construction of the Salford Docks. He was reliable and polite and so later on he was found an office job with the Ship Canal Company and our paths continued to cross. We played a lot of cricket together in those days – occasionally as adversaries, but for two or three seasons rather successfully on the same side. Like me he was a quick bowler, large of hand, tall and lean: a physique he more or less retains to this day. From time to time my work with Booth & Byrne takes me to the Custom House by Number Seven Dock and this is where I will generally find him: these days he wears an impressive uniform commensurate with his senior position with His Majesty's Customs and Excise. Off duty, and strictly for the benefit of his most discreet friends, he has an entertaining collection of stories of attempted bribery, stowaways and all manner of smuggling.

His favourite tale, which he told more often than he really needed to, involved a young fellow from Salford, a dock worker who for any number of reasons had been sacked from his job. Shawcross would mention one or all of absenteeism, pilfering and swearing at an overseer. He called the lad Dudley the Dull-wit yet insisted he was telling a true story. Dudley had had enough of life in Manchester. He stowed away on a cargo ship bound for America. Hiding in a dark hold waiting for the vessel to sail, he fell asleep. He woke up some time later, hungry, thirsty and with no idea of how many days he had slept. The ship's engine was stilled. Hearing movement above decks, he recognised the sounds of dockside activity. He crept out of his hiding place, nonchalantly assumed the role of a crew member, found the nearest gangplank and, his heart thumping with excitement, set foot on land. The Promised Land. Land Dudley thought was New York, but which turned out to be no further from Salford than Huskisson Dock in Liverpool.

Ada was invited to supper too, of course, but she had decided in recent years, with some justification I suppose, that she found Shawcross bumptious: a word I have only ever heard my wife use. It was an epithet I always associate with her, for she used it often to describe the chairman of the old lawn tennis club and even on occasion in reference to her own dear father. This is not to mention Mr Tetlow, the choirmaster at St Hilda's for whom Ada grudgingly plays piano accompaniment. Anyway, she was unable to share a table with the Shawcrosses that evening, she said, having a prior engagement, fortuitously, with a neighbour who had asked her to join her at a performance of chamber music at the Church of St Mary in Hulme.

Mrs Shawcross had seemed distracted all evening and was late in serving the food. In the meantime, over a beer or two, Jeremiah and I covered a multitude of subjects in our conversation – several, it had to be said, fairly boisterously and from positions of near-ignorance. Nevertheless, when the hot-pot arrived it was delicious and the time passed most agreeably. Rather surprisingly, cigars were produced at one point and my friend was moved to open a bottle of American bourbon whisky, which he swore was most definitely not seized contraband.

It was close to midnight. I concede that I was slightly drunk. I was striding down Ordsall Lane towards the docks, in and out of the small pools of illumination cast by the sparse and feeble streetlamps. Yellow patches of light were diffused from the windows and open doorway of the Trafalgar, a notorious public house on the corner of one of the side streets that fanned away from the Lane. I say notorious perhaps unfairly. I have had no dealings with the landlord and have no personal evidence of the establishment's night-time economy, but people do talk of exchanges in stolen goods, of a meeting place for one of Salford's criminal gangs, of a hotbed (if you will forgive the pun) of the area's trade in prostitution.

As I quickened my steps in order to pass by the ale house at a brisk pace, I was stopped in my tracks by the sight of a familiar figure standing in the doorway as if he was waiting to meet somebody. He wore a wide-brimmed hat but his distinctive profile was quite clear in the lamplight: it was Sidney Mulloy. I was less than twenty yards from him and about to address him, when two other men, their heads covered by hoods, emerged from inside the building and engaged him in earnest conversation. I stepped into the shadows and observed. Mulloy now had his back to me as the taller of his interlocutors placed a hand on his shoulder in a gesture that could be construed as either companionable or somewhat threatening. It was his left hand, I noticed, which was decorated with a tattooed image of a bird, perhaps a swallow, swooping above his thumb. The shorter man was doing most of the talking, intently yet soberly, and far too quietly for me to hear a word. After a minute or two the three of them moved away from the doorway and, leaving the Trafalgar behind, they followed the Lane towards the Egerton Mill. My route home was down Woden Street and over the river by the footbridge, but curiosity has a power of its own. At a discreet distance I followed, ignoring the advances of a pair of street girls who had spotted me from the other pavement.

Mulloy was walking between the two strangers, their pace was steady. It crossed my mind that there might be some coercion involved, which gave me another reason to keep them in my sights. They passed the heavy gates to the great sprawl of the dye works, then on beyond the looming dark bulk of Egerton Mill, suddenly disappearing into the yard of the chemical works. Had the gates been unlocked? Here the streetlamps petered out and the space was shadowy and indistinct. The men had disappeared. I had never been inside this yard before and I struggled to gain a sense of what was in front of me: several dark buildings, some of up to three storeys, a towering chimney, and an open cobbled space where empty waggons were lined up alongside stacks of large wooden crates.

Just at that moment I heard sounds of a scuffle: shoe leather scraping on concrete, then sharp, loud breaths, and a stifled cry for help. A sensible man might have retreated at this stage, or at the very least have remained hidden in the shadows. But I bolted forward towards the sounds, round the back of what looked like a warehouse. There in the moon's half-light, I saw the men: they were locked together in a kind of physical stalemate: one man, his wide-brimmed hat falling to the ground, was vainly struggling against the firm grip of a second, both grunting and twitching like a wounded four-legged beast. The third, the taller man, had pulled himself free and suddenly he was holding what looked like a knife; with a deft action he aimed it at his victim's neck. I heard a groan, a shrill cry, and saw the swift lateral movement of the blade. Mulloy, for it was surely he, was left to fall, left to shake, to quiver on the ground, his hands at his savaged throat until his body shuddered, then lay limp and lifeless. Only the panting of the shorter man broke the silence of the dreadful scene before me.

I could not believe my eyes. Then, alarmingly, the shorter man looked up to where I was standing. In my stupor I had wandered into view.

"Hey!" he shouted, and the other man spun round in my direction.

I turned and ran as quickly as I could through the yard, out by the open gates and into the dark lane. I was no more than thirty yards ahead of my pursuers, and their footsteps, ever more rapid, ever more desperate, rang louder and louder in my ears. I could have retraced my steps to the Trafalgar but I chose the opposite direction, rattling all the way down the echoey lane, past the lodge of the soap works, on past the high brick wall which enclosed the vast site of the paper mill. Still I could hear the pair galloping behind me, surely gaining ground, their cries distinct:

"Stop, ya bastard!"

"We're on to ya!"

At the end of Ordsall Lane I darted left, heading for where the Irwell became the waterway housing the Pomona Docks. This was the prospect I could see from my office window: a strip of wharf running along the back sides of the mills and factories I had just scurried past. There were odd nooks in the walls, pontoons attached to the shore, crates stacked high by the water's edge – places which my fevered mind suggested I might hide. As I followed the path, again to the left, the footway stretched ahead of me, a straight line lit here and there by the glow of a ship or two docked on the far side of the flat, inky lagoon in which the lights were perfectly reflected. A few of the taller cranes seemed to reach to the heavens, monuments of geometry, their spindly silhouettes even darker than the sky. The sound of scampering footsteps was still behind me, but for that very brief moment, those five or six seconds, I was out of their sight. I tried to catch my breath. If I carried on running they would see me, they would catch me before I had time to find a hiding place. I looked down to the torpid, black skin of the water and saw a ladder clamped to the brickwork, its metal rungs descending below the surface. My heart was pounding like a steam pump, my sense of reasoning shaken to a blur. I started a prayer, thanking the Lord that we were not in the middle of winter, then jumped on to the ladder, danced down its ten feet of length and, taking a gulp of air into my lungs, submerged myself beneath the surface of the canal. The shock of cold water made me gasp, made my body shiver, but to the two men whose muffled voices I could still hear somewhere above me, I was invisible.

For ten seconds I held my breath, then twenty, eyes shut, in an eerie, watery silence. Then thirty seconds. Thirty-five. Suddenly I had to empty my lungs: I held on until I felt faint, then in desperation I lifted myself up the ladder as surreptitiously as I could. I sucked in the air like a glutton. My ears were full of water, my eyes blinking in the dark. Mercifully, as far as I could tell, the voices had stopped. I waited, my head barely above the surface, my body dangling in the water like a soggy bundle of laundry. Motionless, I waited and waited, my limbs becoming numb, yet ready at any moment to lower my head once more if I heard footsteps. None came. Minutes passed: two, three, it could have been ten. I guessed they had headed along the wharf side expecting to find me cowering in the shadows of one of the kinks in the walls.

Slowly I climbed up the ladder and regained the quay, shaking, blowing like a split plug valve, one eye still on the pathway. Now I was glad of the darkness. After a moment I darted back to the main road and, deciding to take the long way home, crossed the railway line on to Chester Road. There was no sign of the men. Less than ten minutes later I turned into Isabella Street, wondering how to explain my soaking clothes to Ada, my mind also returning to the image of Mulloy, my friend and colleague, scared witless and squirming in the dark, throat cut open, finally an abandoned corpse. I had witnessed a murder. I had a duty to report everything about the last hour to the police, but first of all I needed to try to explain it all to myself.

Sure enough, Mulloy's body was discovered at first light by a storeman at the chemical works.

I had barely slept. I had given myself little chance to suffer nightmares, the conscious echoes of the terrible events revisited my restless mind instead. I saw the dawn break, I heard the birds awakening, and when I had had enough of tossing and turning under the bedsheets, I came downstairs like a ghost. With a pile of wet clothes draped by the kitchen door like an uninvited visitor, Ada and I could not avoid our own investigation over an uneasy breakfast. I held nothing back from her. I had no reason to.

"You must let the police know exactly what happened," she insisted. "Can you remember what the two of them looked like? You must tell them what you saw, Charlie."

"I will," I agreed, resolved to make a telephone call from my office the moment I arrived.

Once at Booth & Byrne, I skipped up to the first floor but not without first pausing to cast a glance into the accounts division where I vainly hoped to see Mulloy at his desk, a cigarette smouldering in his ashtray; he would look up and I would hear his voice – *Mornin', Charlie!* – and it would be perfectly clear that the previous evening had been nothing but a terrible dream. The ground-floor space was almost deserted: two clerks were in early but my friend's desk was unoccupied, the ashtray wiped clean, his chair pushed hard in against its edge – closed for business.

The first thing I noticed when I unlocked the door to my office was a large buff envelope on the carpet inside. I closed the door firmly behind me and stooped to pick it up. It was addressed simply with my surname in black ink and in a hand I recognised. I took it over to my desk, opened it and discovered two loose pages. The first was a letter, the contents of which I greedily devoured:

Dear Charlie,

If you are reading this without my interception then the worst has happened, believe me.

Things are not exactly as they seem, and I do apologise for that. Although I am able to make a decent stab at book-keeping, my work with Booth & Byrne has been a cover. I work for the security services on behalf of the British Government. My mission is sensitive and yesterday I had to expedite matters to maintain my integrity with the target operation. It was a delicate situation and may well have gone wrong.

You will, I have no doubt, be puzzled by what I have just written. Please be assured, Charlie, that although much of my work involves subterfuge, there was NO deception in our friendship, which I have genuinely valued. Indeed, as the mission has taken a turn for the worse, you are the only person I find I can trust. THE ONLY PERSON.

The sheet enclosed shows details of what I believe is a shipment of arms destined for Ireland and specifically for the Irish Volunteer Force. It must be stopped. You would be doing your patriotic duty by alerting the customs authorities (HMCE), but NOT the police, and NOBODY else at Booth & Byrne. I don't know who is implicated in this plot but there has to be somebody, somebody for whom traitor is not too strong a word.

Believe me, Charlie, you are the only one I can trust.

Be bold, my friend,

Mull

I realised I was shaking. I sat down and took a moment to digest what I had read. Then I started at the top line and read the whole letter again. *It was a delicate situation and may well have gone wrong.* Once again I saw in my mind's eye the blade at his throat, that lethal glint in the darkness. Mulloy was a secret agent, a government spy. That was the same conclusion Ada had come to about Violet. Once again the doubts about their marriage reared up. Did Violet already know that her "husband" had been murdered? Why wasn't *she* someone he could trust? *Charlie, you are the only one.* Why was *he* the only one? Why couldn't he trust Pollitt, for example, or a contact in the police?

The Irish Volunteer Force. They were the supporters of Patrick Pearse, the men behind the Easter Rising, a force determined to rid Ireland of British rule. Had I heard an Irish accent in the voices in the night? *We're on to ya!* Was that my imagination realigning a memory to the facts in the letter? *A shipment of arms.* This was a dangerous business. What on earth did Sidney Mulloy, a dead man, expect me to do?

I told hold of the second page. It was a freight docket for the *Blarney Castle*, a merchant ship registered in Liverpool, due to leave Pomona in two days' time. The cargo seemed perfectly unremarkable: mainly large rolls of cotton cloth, footwear, sacks of flour and, twice underlined in pencil, crates of fishing rods. One hundred and ten fishing rods. And associated tackle, also twice underlined. It struck me that the number one hundred and ten corresponded to twice the number of rifles, fifty-five, reported stolen from the Bury barracks of the Lancashire Fusiliers a month or so earlier. At the time a flippant comment within the quartermaster's statement to the newspapers had chimed with me. *Eleven cases with five guns in each,* he had confirmed. *They'd not taken ten, but eleven: one for each member of their cricket team.*

Meanwhile, for "associated tackle", I read ammunition.

The fishing equipment had as its origin a code number SG088-Y15 which I was able to cross-reference from the files in my cabinet. It did not take me long to discover the company name: Smith & Son Sporting Goods of Bradford, West Riding of Yorkshire. Fifteen was the year the business joined our list, 1915. Only one year ago, yet I had never heard of them. It was certainly not a contract that I had signed off. I called in Mr Dewsbury for a brief word; he too had never come across them before.

"If the name has eluded you, Mr Knott," he said, "then it must have been validated at a higher level."

I kept Mulloy's paperwork away from his line of vision.

"At an *even* higher level," he added, an adjustment to curry favour.

"Thank you, Mr Dewsbury," I said, without looking up. He knew to withdraw.

The *Blarney Castle* was a name I was familiar with: it was a ship which sailed irregularly between Manchester and Dublin. I opened a ledger on my desk and checked the details of the week's departures. I found it without delay: she was berthed at Number Three Dock and her captain's name was Moore.

I turned to Mulloy's letter again. *Alert the customs authorities (HMCE), but NOT the police, and NOBODY else at Booth & Byrne.* At my hand sat my telephone. Ten minutes earlier I had come up to my office with the firm intention of contacting the police. I had witnessed a murder. I had details that might lead to an arrest. The Trafalgar on Ordsall Lane. Around midnight. Two men. One tall, one not so tall. A swallow tattoo. Maybe an Irish accent. For the moment, however, I decided to take Mulloy's advice to keep everything I had discovered to myself.

Later that morning Mr Dewsbury helped me locate all the records of shipping movements under the agency of Booth & Byrne within the previous two years. I thanked him once more and carried the stack of files into my office where I could peruse them in private. The *Blarney Castle* had crossed the Irish Sea from the port of Manchester on four occasions in 1914, each time with a similar cargo on board: textiles, foodstuffs, clothing, light machinery. I studied the dockets carefully, matching quantities with weights, and quickly found a discrepancy. In two shipments, two months apart, were similar batches of ladies' dresses, crated and dispatched from a factory in north Manchester. The weight of the second batch was considerably heavier than the first, but without the direct comparison this would raise no concern.

I racked my brains to remember the chronology of that year, the summer the war broke out, but more pertinently, the summer that the government passed the Irish Home Rule bill, rejected amendments to it, then suspended it until the war was over. It was at that time, I recalled, that there had been a theft of rifles and ammunition from the Cheshire Regiment's garrison at Chester Castle. Perhaps I was jumping to the same conclusions as Mulloy, this time on a hunch rather than by any serious work of detection: the earlier cargo of the *Blarney Castle*, sailing from Pomona to Dublin on Thursday 30th July 1914, had included armaments in boxes falsely labelled as containing fashionable frocks.

*

If there was one person I could trust it was Jeremiah Shaw-cross. Bumptious he may have been, but he was a Method-ist lay preacher, a man of great integrity and utterly scrupu-lous in his work. I was on the point of making a telephone call to his office at the Custom House when I remembered what Ada had said about Violet. *She works in the telephone exchange, doesn't she? Listening in to people's conversations.* I had no idea of the woman's part in all this but I made the decision to leave Cornbrook Road, and strode directly past the sight of the *Blarney Castle* herself – sedately moored up, wisps of smoke gently rising from her funnel – and up the Trafford Road to the Custom House.

I did not mention the name of Mulloy on speaking to Shawcross, but the sight of the dockets and the insistence in my manner convinced him that he should act.

"When she's loaded up an' ready to sail," he declared, "I'll have some o' my officers step aboard for a random inspec-tion. The fishin' rods, you say, Charlie?"

"Aye, them," I said. "But they'll not be rods, they'll be rifles."

And indeed they were.

Two days later, shortly after dawn, the ship was raided. Fif-ty-five Lee Enfield rifles were lifted from their crates along with hundreds of rounds of ammunition. It was reported to me that Captain Moore pleaded innocence, but his quarters were vigorously searched ("ransacked" was the word Shaw-cross preferred) and documents were seized which included a note of validation to a known alias of the Irish Volunteer Force on Booth & Byrne stationery. Subjected to physical threats (omitted from the official HMCE report, I assume) and given the option of leniency if he divulged the origin of the note, Moore took little time in offering up the name of Martyn Byrne, Chairman of the Board and, it appeared, an Irish republican sympathiser.

The very same day, my employer was arrested by officers of the Salford Constabulary just as he was finishing his lunch in the company of incredulous business associates at the Midland Hotel in the centre of Manchester.

6

Dearest Mother and Father,

Thank you for your letter. I'm glad that you are having a fair summer. You should get away to the seaside if you can. I'm sure Father is due a week off from B&B.

At last we are having four days' leave in Amiens. It's a lovely town with some fine architecture. There are times when you can't hear the guns at all from here and you forget that men are trying to kill each other less than twenty miles away. Someone arranged a football match against the local French. I ended up playing (don't laugh, Father). I played goalkeeper and actually did alright! I might even join a team when we get back home from this rotten war.

There's talk of a big charge soon but for now, at least, I can relax. I bumped into a couple of pals I trained with. They're both called Alfred, so there's three of us. We're all musical so we're writing some sketches and songs and will put on a bit of a show for the rest of the lads. Alf is one of the two brothers from Stockport, and Alfie is a bit older. He's a music teacher from Leeds. We call ourselves the Three Alfs. I still insist on Alfred, you'll be pleased to know, Mother.

That's all for now.

I'll write again when I get the chance.

All my love,

Alfred

*

In the stately office on the second floor of Booth & Byrne was a large portrait in oils of the founders of the company. They stood side by side in the picture, shaking hands, behind a polished wooden table upon which sat a lovingly-created model of a mid-nineteenth century tea clipper. Both men offered a hint of a smile, giving an impression of confidence or self-satisfaction. It was a fairly recent painting, commissioned a year or two before Mr Booth's unexpected death, and the faces of these two most successful Mancunians invited you to gaze into their twinkling eyes and share in their achievements.

All of which was most disconcerting as it hung on the wall behind Byrne's wide desk, at which now sat Osmund Pollitt. He had asked me a direct question and yet I was distracted, not for the first time, by the artwork. A bottle of Scotch whisky had been opened and we were drinking, he insisted, to toast my success in foiling a plot against the British state. It seemed far too grand a description for my contribution but I did appreciate a generous glass of such a fine single malt, even at ten o'clock in the morning.

"No, Osmund, you're right," I said presently. "I'd no idea what Mulloy was up to. He kept his work, well, his secret work, and our friendship very separate."

"He had professional standards," agreed Pollitt.

"How much did you know about him? Really."

My boss took a sip of scotch and slowly savoured its taste, deciding, I imagined, what to say and what to hold back.

"Well, I did know he was an agent. One of Kell's boys."

"Kell?"

"Vernon Kell. You've not heard of him, Charlie? He runs what they call 'an intelligence service' out of London. Protecting the realm and all that. Sniffing out traitors, subversives, Germans, IVF. It's part of the war effort, I've no doubt."

"Was Mulloy actually from Liverpool? All that stuff about his father gettin' shot durin' the strikes?"

"Yes, I think that was true. I've no reason to believe it wasn't. I don't know everything, by any means. I was approached by the Chief Constable at the start of it all. You know, to engage him here, give him a free run. I was told there and then that there were suspicions about weapons leaving from Manchester. They wanted a man at the docks."

I picked up my glass and drank a little. The painting behind Pollitt's head again drew my attention.

"And Mr Byrne?" I said, unsure of exactly how to frame a question.

Pollitt turned slightly in his seat, following my gaze over his shoulder.

"Oh, I knew absolutely nothing about him."

He faced me again, disbelief in his expression.

"The sporting goods business in Bradford was a fiction he'd created. A ghost client. The address turned out to be the premises of a barber's shop. I still can't credit it. I knew he had Irish family, you know, way back – Belfast, I think – but he never spoke to me about politics. I never had an impression that he was under suspicion. But it seems like Mulloy had gained the confidence of the smugglers. Then something must have changed. Maybe he was betrayed, maybe he was clumsy, made a mistake."

The gruesome tableau of the moonlit yard at the chemical works flashed up once again. Pollitt was still speaking, slowly, deliberately:

"I imagine his plan was to do just as you did, Charlie. Wait until the guns were on board before having them seized. Or perhaps arrange to have the ship raided in Dublin."

"Somehow he was betrayed," I agreed. "Or else he was never really trusted in the first place. Why would he say I were th'only one he could trust? Why not his wife? Well, I say wife. Violet, whoever she really was."

"Oh, she was on his team, Charlie. I was told they came as a couple. I don't know if they got married or not. Once he was compromised, once he wrote you that note, then the last thing he would do was implicate her. He would be trained to keep her at arm's length, I imagine. Break the link. Maintain her professional integrity, I think is the expression. You'll not be seeing her again, that's for sure."

"She'll be back in Hertfordshire."

"Hertfordshire?"

"Aye. Never mind. It was part of her story. Her fairy story. Ada'll be sorry, mind. She'd made a pal, I think. She wanted to make a suffragist out of her."

Pollitt smiled.

"And you'll not be seeing those two thugs again, I've no doubt."

"I wouldn't wish to."

"What was it you said? A tattoo?"

"Aye, a bird, like a swallow, on his left hand. I described him the best I could, you know, to the constable. Tall, slim, built like a seam bowler. You know what I mean."

Pollitt drained his glass.

"Well, Charlie, him and his mate, they'll be a long way from Manchester, believe you me. They'll probably be back in Ireland now, under cover somewhere, hidden away and well out of reach."

7

Dear Mother, Dear Father,

I trust you are keeping well. I hope you get this letter soon but it's all a bit chaotic at the moment. The supply lines are not so reliable.

The advances we made were short-lived and expensive. We lost many men, many pals. I'm sorry to say we lost Alfie. He stepped on a mine. I'm alright, don't fret about me, I'm looking after myself. What was left of our unit was holed up in farm buildings for days sniping at Fritz until we were ordered to withdraw. I'm back where I started two weeks ago and our positions are being pounded by artillery most of the time. The front trenches are dreadful. We are a right old mix now. Reinforcements join us from all different regiments: Irish, Scots, Northumberland.

It rains for hours and freezes at night. We've seen a bit of snow falling in flurries. For days I have worn wet socks inside wet boots. I daren't take them off for fear of seeing what my feet look like. Nobody can stay warm. Hot food rarely reaches us from the support. Thank God for tea and cigarettes.

Thank you for the parcel you sent and your nice letter. It was lovely to read your news of home but I was upset to hear about Grandfather. I shared the cake (it was still nice and moist) but I kept the tin of ham for myself.

It would be nice to think that the fighting will end soon but it just seems like a dead end.

That's all I have room for. I cadged this page from an Irishman called Pat.

Sending you my love,

Alfred

Winter announced itself in Salford by way of a heavy overnight snowfall at the end of the month of November.

"It makes you think of Christmas," exclaimed Ada as she drew back the curtains and gazed in wonder at the transformed scene the length of Isabella Street.

For one morning at least the roads and pavements were thick with snow, and folk of a certain disposition became playful on their way to work. The fluffy white drifts quickly lost their appeal, however, turning grey and skiddy, then brown and slushy, and finally murky and puddled as hundreds of boots squelched through them. The clouds remained dark all day long, promising more precipitation but none came and, mercifully, neither did a pernicious frost.

It seemed that the bad weather had affected everybody's schedule. People arrived late for work, myself included – wrapped up in my thick coat and winter gloves – and some even used the conditions as an excuse for absenteeism. Deliveries were delayed, lunches taken early, routines upended. What little activity there was at the docks was running in a haphazard manner that was quite disconcerting.

One happy consequence of such unpredictability was a chance meeting with Daniel Harrop on my way home at the end of the afternoon. The daylight had faded by four o'clock and, having nothing of import left to do, I decided to leave the office early. I could only assume he had taken advantage of a similar situation, and we found ourselves tramping towards each other by Throstle Nest.

"How do, Danny!" I shouted, catching his eye.

"Charlie! Good to see you," he replied. "It's been a while."

"Aye, it has. What a day, then, eh? Everythin' at half speed, an' all for a bit o' snow."

"Aye, it were a devil gettin' down here this mornin'. I were on th'early shift."

"Oh, I thought you might have been sent home early this afternoon."

"No, this is me normal time if I start early doors. They'll not be finishin' early at Ford's. They dunna give no leeway, believe you me. It's a tight ship, an' no mistake."

Danny was fidgeting with the strap on his duffel bag, his hands part-covered in grimy, fingerless gloves. In the glow of the gaslight I noticed that his thick moustache had started to grey at the edges. As for my own signs of mortality, I had taken to wearing a navy blue corduroy cap outdoors to cover my alarmingly receding hairline.

"How's your Flora?" I asked

"Flora? She's well. Can't grumble."

"She's still out an' about with – what did you call it? – her circle, is she?"

"Her circle, aye," he said, a half-smile forming on his lips.

"You know, we've still not met her, have we? We've never had the pleasure, Ada an' me."

"I can't rightly remember, Charlie."

We had fallen into a steady walk together, heading towards the station side by side.

"No, well, we've not. Never met. I reckon it's about time we did."

From I knew not quite where, other than perhaps from Ada's comment about the morning's snowscape, I had the sudden thought to mention Christmas.

"I tell you what, Danny. How about you two joinin' us for Christmas Day? Share dinner with us. We can have a bit of a party."

"Christmas?"

His scarf had come unloose. I waited while he twisted it into a knot around his throat.

"Aye, Christmas Day. You got owt else planned?"

"Well, no. No, I dunna suppose we have. Nowt that I know of, any road."

"Well, then. It'd cheer us up, that's the honest truth of it. We'll not have our Alfred with us this year."

"No, course you'll not. How's he doin', your lad? Do you get much news?"

"He writes now an' again. As much as he can, I'm sure."

"There's half o' the lads at Ford's over in France now, I reckon. We've got young lasses on the lines doin' men's work."

"Well, our Alfred's says he's copin'. It must be hell, an' I'm sure we don't know the half of it, but he's a strong lad. He says he's copin', Danny, so I reckon he is. I reckon he must be."

"It's got to be tough for you an' all. Both o' you."

"Aye, it is. Especially for his mother."

"Aye."

"So, it'll just be us an' Ada's mother, if she can manage it. For Christmas Day. You know we lost her father a month or two back. Quite sudden…"

"No. No, I'm sorry, Charlie. I didn't know that."

"No, well, there's no reason why you should have heard. It was his heart."

We were approaching the station, mixing with a gathering crowd of workers, all eager to get off home and into the warm.

"I hope the trains are runnin' better than they were this mornin'," said Danny, lifting his bag onto his shoulder.

"So?"

"So?"

"About Christmas? Would you be our guests, then?"

"It's very nice o' you to ask me, Charlie. To ask us both…"

"So, you'll mention it to Flora, will you, an' let me know? You can call in on your way home some time, can't you? Just pop in an' let one of us know if you're comin'."

"Aye, I can. I can do that, Charlie. It's very kind."

"An' you don't think you've got owt else planned?"

"Well, I've not. I can't think I have. I can't say for the wife, mind."

It had begun to drizzle, a cold spray in the pitiless air, more like sleet. Danny pulled up the collar on his jacket, tightened his scarf again. We shook hands and I patted him on the elbow as we parted.

"Take care, Danny," I called. "An' keep warm, an' all. See you again soon, eh?"

"Aye, you too," he shouted back. "Give me love to your Ada, won't you?"

He smiled and was gone, melting into the mist, lost amongst the shifting shapes and shadows.

In spite of the earnest efforts of the Police Prosecutor, Martyn Byrne avoided conviction on the charges of supplying illegal arms and subversion. In his defence, his lawyers argued that the evidence against him was largely circumstantial and that the documentation was not to be entirely trusted. There were claims of forgery and an anti-Irish conspiracy. The week before Christmas the man walked free: vindicated, he insisted to a crowd of journalists, but not unscathed. In the weeks that followed many of his business associates and concerned allies, not to mention other wise men of authority who had his ear, advised him to step down from his position in the company of Booth & Byrne: he was sixty-three years old, his reputation was damaged but not ruined, and he ought to resign with his pride intact, retire even, sell off a chunk of his shares, let the next generation take up the reigns.

And this is exactly what he did. By the end of January young Mr Booth, Jacob, son of Jonathan, had assumed the chairmanship of the company. I was astounded to be offered the fellow's previous position managing operations in Liverpool, but it took me no time at all to graciously decline. Perhaps sensing that goodwill towards him was suddenly in short supply amongst the traders of England's north-west, Mr Byrne withdrew into the shadows. About six months later, along with his wife, he left the country to retire in the

United States of America. In Boston, Massachusetts, to be accurate.

The company was renamed the Phoenix (Port of Manchester) Shipping Agency Limited (formerly Booth & Byrne) – a rather ungainly title in my view – and under this guise we continued to do our business. The drama was all too much for Mr Horridge in accounts, who had indeed been re-engaged as the division was losing much of its personnel to the war effort. The old man was of a mind to retire for a second and final time. The long-time stalwart of Booth & Byrne (apparently, his wife had been part of the same chapel choir as Mr Booth's good lady when they were girls) now felt utterly unable to manage such an upheaval.

As for myself, I never doubted my employer's guilt. Nor could I forgive him for his part, however oblique, in the death of my friend Sidney Mulloy. Beyond the framed portrait which remained hanging in the sanctum on the second floor, the face of Martyn Byrne was never seen again in the offices on Cornbrook Road, which was perhaps just as well.

And so the dust finally settled on the *Blarney Castle* affair. The police investigation into the murder of Mulloy reached a dead end. I was interviewed more than once: firstly in my office as a witness, and secondly, in a nondescript building on a street off Piccadilly where I had the feeling that I was being treated, however briefly, as a suspect. Further to which, Jeremiah Shawcross vouched for my presence in Ordsall at midnight on the night in question. A statement from one of the street girls who had seen me in the Lane I could dismiss as being inconsequential. Witnesses from those in the Trafalgar at the time were so vague as to be useless. Ada, supervisor of our domestic laundry arrangements, was asked to corroborate my story of submersion in the filthy waters of the Ship Canal. *But why, Mr Knott, did you not contact the police at the earliest opportunity to report the murder?* I believe the intervention of Osmund Pollitt behind the scenes finally got the investigators off my back. With a glimpse into the politics of the case, detectives were left in the end with a victim and a motive, but no trace of a suspect to arrest, no murderer to put behind bars.

Christmas had long been my wife Ada's favourite time of the year. She admitted that, being an only child, her parents had probably used the occasion to indulge her more than ever. These days she yielded to all its rituals and traditions with gusto, from the carolling and the sending of cards and gifts, to the food and decorations that embellished our home.

This year, in spite of shortages of certain items on the markets, she was determined to make a special effort. The tree was always the centrepiece, standing in all its glory by the sitting-room window. She insisted that I buy the most fragrant little pine I could find for sale on the docks, and then spent hours decking its branches with coloured ribbon, teased cotton wool, gingerbread, shiny paper stars, tiny plaster figurines and, here and there, carefully poised miniature candles which she would light at dusk. For our table she ordered a goose from a renowned butcher's shop in the centre of Manchester. She wrote more greetings cards than ever, both to very best friends and to neighbours she hardly knew. As usual she was invited to several carol concerts but whereas in the past she could be rather particular as to which ones she chose to attend, this year she went to every one without a second thought.

I knew the reasons for her enthusiastic embrace of the season, more festive and sociable than ever. The absence of our brave son, for a start, and the death of her dear father, made this year's event one of great poignancy for us both, and especially so for Ada.

We received plenty of cards in return, several containing condolences. One notable missing example was Mr Byrne's. It had been a company tradition that every single member of staff, from directors to office cleaners, was sent a Christmas card signed personally by the chairman. But not so this year.

When the twenty-fifth arrived, Ada rose early to prepare the bird. By the middle of the morning, once the rain had eased, once the feeble sun peeked out, we decided to take a little fresh air. The streets round about were quiet. We walked as far as Hullard Park, deciding against a seat, so bitter was the wind. What crossed my mind was an imagined winter scene in northern France: I wondered about the tempera-tures in those wretched trenches, wondered about the sort of Christmas Day Alfred was enduring. Would the shelling be paused? Would the day be blessed with peace and good-will, and a decent hot meal? In some draughty bunker with a damp greatcoat buttoned up to his throat, would our son be warm enough? As we turned to retrace our steps, I tightened my grip on Ada's gloved hand, and stooped to kiss her cheek. We shared a sad smile. Somehow, I knew that she had been thinking the very same thoughts as me.

Just as we were leaving the park, we met Mr Tetlow, the choirmaster at St Hilda's. Here was a fellow for whom the word bumptious was invented, my wife had said to me more than once; after doing his bidding on the piano with a strained smile on her face, after patiently putting up with his histrionics, she regularly came home seething. I had never met the man before.

"A merry Christmas to you both!" he called.

Wrapped in a black topcoat and with a fancy silk scarf around his neck, he was slowly pushing a wheelchair over the gravel pathway between the damp lawns. A poorly-looking old woman sat slumped in the seat, her head covered by a floppy woollen hat and her body reduced to a formless mass lost under shawls and blankets. Her eyes were closed.

"And to you, Mr Tetlow," replied Ada warily.

"This is Mr Knott, I presume," said the man to my wife, whilst offering me his hand to shake.

"Yes, it is. This is my husband – Charlie. We were just out taking some fresh air before our meal."

"I believe you're with Booth & Byrne, are you not, sir?"

"That's right."

Beneath his bowler, his ruddy face was edged with sandy whiskers grown white at the chin.

"I imagine maritime trade is suffering like everything else," he said, "isn't it, with the country at war?"

"Aye, it's not a good time to be in the shippin' business."

"I had a marvellous view of Pomona Docks when I worked at Tatton Mills. A big comfortable office on the second floor. I was the private secretary to one of the processing managers. A lovely fellow. Meticulous, you know? I'm at the hospital now, as I think your wife is aware. She may very well have mentioned the fact to you. No? The one in Salford. It's a job in administration, so I am allowed to shine."

"Well, I hope you have a happy Christmas Day," said Ada, with a tone of finality in her voice.

"What do you think of my scarf, Mr Knott?" Mr Tetlow asked, lovingly fingering the material at his throat. "It's very fine, don't you think? Pure silk. A gift to myself. I spotted it in a shop window in town and, well, I couldn't resist."

"It's very smart," I said. "Bold colours."

"Come along, Charlie," insisted Ada abruptly. "We need to get along. We have guests, Mr Tetlow."

"Well, you two have a pleasant afternoon, won't you? Very nice to have met you, Mr Knott."

As we left him strolling with his passenger towards the empty bowling green, it occurred to me that he had not introduced the lady in the wheelchair.

"Was his mother asleep, do you think?" I asked Ada.

"She might have been," she answered, striding homewards. "It wasn't his mother, by the way. It's his wife."

"Really?"

"Yes. It's a sad story in its way. He brings her to choir practice sometimes. Parks her in a corner where she can watch and listen."

"His wife? She's much older than him."

"I don't think she is, in fact, Charlie. She's got some incurable wasting disease. One of the ladies said poliomyelitis."

"That *is* sad."

"Well, of course it is. He does encourage sympathy amongst members of the choir, though. And it doesn't stop him being conceited and, well, bumptious."

She laughed at herself, knowing I would have something to say about her overuse of the word.

"He is a bit, in't he?"

"And you notice how he addressed all his comments, all his interest towards you? That's because you're a man. He has so little respect for women and yet without us his precious choir would just be one unreliable tenor, two pretty feeble baritones and a bass who can't concentrate on anything for more than ten seconds."

I had to smile. We ambled back home arm in arm, the sun's work done for the day, the grey clouds threatening rain.

Ada's mother appeared at Isabella Street shortly before noon in a taxicab. She was the only guest at our feast. A week earlier a rather lovely Christmas card had been delivered: a square design with the wording *Christmas Joys Be Thine* decorated with painted images of holly and ivy. Inside was written a sentence or two in black ink in a scratchy hand which I did not recognise:

> *Thank you for your invitation but we will not be able to join you at your home on Christmas Day. Flora's sister is not well and we are to visit her for the holiday. She lives in Pendlebury. I hope you have a lovely day. From Daniel and Flora.*

Part Five
1917

1

Dear Mother, Dear Father,

Thank you for your letters. Forgive me for not writing back so quickly every time. You can imagine that conditions are not easy and my news is not so cheery in any case.

It's been a horrid winter but I think we are past the worst. We have sunnier days now and can dry out our boots. Where the ground is not so churned up there are shoots of new grass and herbs and even a few wild flowers budding already. There's birdsong, too, now and then. There's a nightingale somewhere – you can her chirping in the dark when the guns fall silent. The days are longer but that means that Fritz is more carefree, shooting across the divide whenever he feels like it. It's strange to think that the enemy can probably hear the nightingale too. Nature doesn't pick sides, does it? Anyway, we're ordered to fire back. It's a waste of energy and a waste of ammunition. Our new captain is reckless in my opinion. He reckons the Germans have had enough and will retreat soon.

On the bigger scale this battle is stalled and has been for months. It's part of a front they call the Somme. You'll have read about it, I suppose. Whatever it is you've read, let me tell you it's boredom and discomfort and the odd brush with danger.

There's a couple of us here, once we've done writing letters, we'll start on the poetry. I've started making up some poems. I can't say they're any good but they help me get my thoughts

*straight. The rhythms and the choosing of the words take my
mind off the damp and the hunger and the noise of shell bursts,
all the mess of it.*

I'll write again soon.

With love,

Alfred

We were past the start, floundering somewhere in the
middle, or perhaps even drifting towards the end of what
had turned into a long, global conflict. Trading was desperate, there were shortages of just about every important com-
modity, and prices were generally rising faster than people's
capacity to pay them.

It was in these inauspicious circumstances that Ada's
mother (and, by association, Ada herself) felt obliged to sell
the shops her father had so proudly established in happier
times. There was no great windfall, of course, no soft landing for us into a cushion of luxury, but at least the assets did
sell, and more quickly than we had ever hoped. The shop
in Chorlton-cum-Hardy was bought by a local wholesale
butcher who had plans to convert the space into a cold storage depot. The much larger Dooley's Fashion Store in the city
centre, the family's pride and joy, was eventually acquired,
after some intense haggling amongst solicitors, by a direct
competitor in the ladieswear business. The buyer, conscious
of the value of the much-respected brand, agreed to continue
to trade under the Dooley's name, which was some consolation at least to Ada's mother.

Late one Sunday morning in February – one of those
grinding, bitter days when frost's steely grip shows no sign

of loosening, when the warming colours of spring seem hopelessly distant – we had an unexpected visitor. Ada had eschewed her usual attendance at St Hilda's for the cosier comforts of the kitchen hearth, where she had spent a good hour preparing winter vegetables and a small side of beef for our dinner. The sweet aromas already filled the air.

I rose to answer the vigorous knocking at the door and was surprised to find Daniel Harrop on the step, stamping his feet on the ground and rubbing his hands together to stay warm. He had an old woolly hat on his head and a knitted scarf wrapped around his neck, but I pitied him for his coat which looked shabby and unsubstantial. He smiled at me as our eyes met and made to step inside without hesitation.

"Charlie! A happy New Year to you!" were his first words.

"An' you too, Danny," I replied. It was an odd thing for him to say; we had passed New Year's Day several weeks earlier, as I recall. "Come in. Come in an' get yourself warm. This is a surprise."

"Sorry, I'm unannounced."

"Don't worry, lad. We don't stand on ceremony in this house. Come on through. Ada's in the kitchen."

I guided him into the back, took his hat and scarf and sat him down at the table with his knees facing the fireplace.

"Hello, Ada," he said, straightening his hair after a fashion. Though it was now largely grey, he sported the same tousled mop he had always had since he was an urchin of a schoolboy in Gee Cross. "Summat smells good."

"Hello, Danny," said my wife, as much surprised to see him as I was. "Shall I make you some tea?"

"Well, I wouldn't say no, Ada, if you dunna mind. I'm not plannin' on stoppin' long, but a brew'd be grand, ta. It's quite a walk from town."

"You walked it?"

"Aye, I can't be doin' waitin' for trams in this weather. You're better off keepin' movin.'"

"Did you have a nice Christmas, then?" asked Ada, putting the kettle on the stove top.

"Aye. Just quiet, you know."

"And how's Flora? And her sister, of course. Is she better?"

"Aye, she's a bit better, I think."

"And Flora?"

"Flora's very well, thanks. She sends 'er love."

"It was a shame," I said, "you two couldn't get over here for Christmas Day."

"Aye, it were. It were a shame, Charlie. But unavoidable, you know. Any road, how's your Alfred?"

"Alfred? Well, we have to believe he's still in one piece. That's right, in't it, love?"

Ada, busy opening a new packet of tea on the other side of the kitchen, said nothing.

"We had a letter from him this week," I continued. "It seems things are in a lull, you know, fightin' wise, where he is."

"Well, that's a blessin', Charlie."

"Aye, I suppose it is."

Danny leaned forwards in his seat to warm his hands at the glowing coals.

"You've got a nice fire goin', Ada," he said, pulling a handkerchief out of his coat pocket and rubbing his nose with it.

A minute or two later, once he had taken a sip or two of tea, our visitor coughed to clear his throat and addressed us both with a serious look on his face.

"Thank you for the tea, Ada, but this is more than a social call. I've got some news for you both…"

"News?" I interrupted. "What kind o'news?"

"Charlie," Ada said, "let him speak, for goodness' sake."

"As you two are me closest friends," he went on (with a speech I imagined he had partly rehearsed), "I wanted to tell you in person. You know, properly. I have some news."

He paused to take another sip of tea, then looked up at us intently, first Ada then me.

"I'm leavin' Manchester," he declared.

"Leavin'?"

"Aye, leavin'. I'm joinin' up."

"Joinin' up?"

"Charlie, let him finish a sentence!"

Danny smiled and unfastened his coat.

"I'm joinin' up."

"But you don't have to."

Ada glowered at me.

"You've no need. You're not conscription age."

"No, you're right, I'm not. I'm forty-four next. Some would say that's too old to put a soldier's uniform on."

"Aye, well, an' I'd be one of 'em."

"But *I* wouldn't, you see. An' I do believe we have to win this war. I do believe that. Germany 'as to be defeated, Charlie, an' I wanna play me part. Make a proper contribution."

I had stood up by now, rather exasperated. Ada remained at the table listening keenly as he resumed.

"I thought I'd be able to do that here, you know, make a proper contribution. Right here in Trafford Park, at Ford's. I thought they'd have turned to manufacturin' arms by now. Or armoured vehicles. Or even landships. They're makin' 'em in other works, you know, especially in Birmingham and places."

"But not at Ford's?"

"No. Not at Ford's, Ada. It's one o' the biggest, newest production lines in the country but we're not on a war footin'. It's th'Americans, o' course. That's the reason why not. None o' the bosses in America wanna get involved, do they? Stay out of it, that's their thinkin'. Keep their heads down. We all thought they'd change their minds back a year or so ago. You remember *Lusitania*, I'm sure?"

We both nodded.

"An unprotected ocean liner – full of Americans, by the way – hit by a German submarine, sank in less than half an hour. You remember? Crew an' passengers missin' in their hundreds." He picked up his cup and gulped the rest of the tea. "But still no reaction. *The American public is not ready for war*," he said, mimicking the accent. "Ford's just does as it's told, I suppose. We've started makin' ambulances, an' more tractors, new lines startin' up, but nowt military. There's a few of us down there feelin' like we're just kickin' our heels, if you know what I mean."

For no reason, I had moved over to the hearth. I took the poker and gave the coals a rough prod.

"You probably think I'm bein' a fool, I know," said Danny.

"I do admire your commitment," said Ada.

I filled a shovel from the scuttle and scattered fresh coal on to the fire, smothering the flames for a moment until, with a crackle and a puff, flickering fingers of fire began to poke up through the smoky slack.

"What does Flora think?" I asked, turning my gaze back to our visitor.

"Flora? It's nowt to do with her."

"Course it is, Danny. You'd be leavin' 'er behind. With all the worry."

"She understands."

"Does she?"

"We've talked all about it. Flora understands. She's proud o' me, she says. I think old Walter would be proud o' me, an' all."

Ada stood up, straightened her apron and moved over to the stove, where she gave the pans a distracted stir.

"I'll join as a regular volunteer," Danny started up once more. "I'll do me general trainin', whatever they want, then I'll ask to join th'engineers. I want to learn how to fix up the landships. They call it the Tank Regiment. I'd be part o' the mechanicals. I could be useful, Charlie, couldn't I? I'm a bloody good mechanic an' I've allers been a fast learner. I'd be more useful with 'em over there than workin' on a production line in Trafford Park makin' bloody tractors."

I had never seen Danny like this before. So energised. So firm in his conviction. So engaged. I knew there was nothing I could do to change his mind. To be absolutely honest about it, I had no urge to do so and certainly no right to even try.

"Would you like to stay and have some dinner with us, Danny?" asked Ada. "There's bit of beef that'll stretch to three and I've made more than enough vegetables for us two. You do like a roast beef dinner, don't you?"

The man sat up straight and took in a deep breath, filling his nostrils with the smell of gravy.

"Who doesn't, Ada?" he said with a smile. "That's proper nice o' you to ask. An' I'll say yes. Yes, please."

"Charlie can set the table," said Ada. "Can't you, love? Set it for three. And get a beer glass out for our guest."

I smiled, but my mind was uneasy, filled with Danny Harrop's courageous words of duty and battlefield tanks.

"Are you sure you really know what you're doin'?" I asked him.

"Not really," he said grinning. There was a light in his eyes. He had told us what he had come to say and now was relaxed, as self-assured as I had ever seen him. He stood up and rubbed his hands together; he had successfully accomplished a difficult task and his reward was a calm spirit and a plate of beef and vegetables.

"No, not really," he repeated. "Does anybody really know what they're doin'? Especially these days with everythin' turned upside down."

He took a couple of steps towards the stove to address my wife:

"I'd love to stay for dinner, Ada. Thanks. As long as your husband promises not to try an' change me mind. I've made me decision. I wanna be in France in a month or two. Happen before Easter Sunday, all bein' well."

2

Dearest Mother and Father,

I hope this finds you well. I hope you have got over your cold, Mother. Don't let Father scrimp on the coal for the fire. You must keep the house warm.

At last they're moving us. Not backwards, not forwards, but sideways. North from our position here, I think. Probably not so far away, as our business is not done by any means in this blighted corner of France. You'll know about the Russians, I imagine. Some bloody allies they were. Fritzi won't have his eastern front to worry about for much longer, will he? He'll be wanting to break through on the western side and we'll have to do what we can to stop him.

I was carried back to the reserve trenches last week for a night. I had such a head pain and was vomiting. An orderly said it was concussion. Don't worry, I'm alright again now. I'm just telling you in case you think I always keep the worst of it out of my letters.

I've been writing some poems. Did I already tell you? I think most of them are hopeless but I don't really care. I just like trying to get them right. I might send you one or two that I think are worthy. And I'll bring them all back with me when our unit gets its leave granted. It can't be much longer. I've been away for a year already, so I hope they'll let us visit our homes for a week or so fairly soon. I hope it'll be in the summer when the sunshine can make even the ship canal look beautiful.

Thanks for your letters. I read them over and over.
With all my love,
Alfred

I had been reading with increased trepidation the newspaper reports of events in Petrograd, the city whose name before the war was Saint Petersburg, the seat of Russian monarchy; it was thought the old name sounded too Germanic. If there was a feeling of unease in Britain towards our own army's conduct of the war, this was as nothing compared with the deep-rooted anger and resentment amongst the Russian people, not only towards their inept generals but also against what they represented, namely an autocratic tsar and a government run by an entitled elite. For over three hundred years the Romanov family had headed a feudal system whose critics considered it to be strangled by its medieval roots. Aside from the hierarchy of the church and a small bourgeoisie, the population was badly educated and poor, and each winter was a battle against hunger and despair.

In February mass strikes were organised in protest against food rationing, involving hundreds of thousands of workers; inevitably there were violent clashes with members of the police. Later, soldiers were ordered to open fire to disperse huge crowds of demonstrators, but rather than kill civilians they turned their guns on their officers. By early March the government had been overturned and the tsar was prevented from leaving the city. Needless to say, with such chaos erupting in the capital, the war effort against Germany lost its focus.

I have long been interested in the politics of power. What has angered me is how very little of it is in the hands of the common man, and how difficult it is for him to wrest influence from those into whose laps power seems effortlessly to fall – generally through corruption, violence or, most often, an accident of birth.

What was happening in Petrograd seemed to many of the correspondents I read to be only the beginning. For the time being there was an arrangement between a new governing group holding liberal principles and representatives of the old guard: an accommodation whereby Russia remained notionally at war but greater freedoms were promised for its citizens. The sense was that this could not last; this superficial redistribution of power was not the full-blooded revolution the majority of Russians wanted. And in all of the newspaper reports that I read, there had been little mention so far of Vladimir Lenin.

Factionalism was an unavoidable truth in political movements. I saw it in the Labour Party, especially in regards to attitudes towards the war. Alfred would have witnessed it at first hand: the rescinded commands, the shifts in strategy, the juddering redirections amongst the generals of the British army. For years Ada had been aware of the tension between the suffragists and the suffragettes, both groups ostensibly working for the same goals, and now even between members of the same Pankhurst family. In Russia, the principal factions, revolutionary to lesser and greater degrees respectively, were the Mensheviks and the Bolsheviks. Here were two foreign words that would become internationally known by the end of the year.

*

It was somewhat ironic that in the first week in April, around the date that Daniel Harrop had set himself to sail to France as part of British army reinforcements, President Wilson of the United States announced that his country was to declare war on Germany. Quite suddenly Danny's gripes about American neutrality held no water. The Germans had intensified their U-boat attacks in British seas, causing ever more American ships to be torpedoed, ever more American sailors to perish. The enemy calculated that such collateral damage was a risk worth taking to strangle supply lines to our country, believing that the American politicians lacked resolve, and that their military was weak and poorly resourced. Whatever the case, Ada and I rejoiced in what we considered to be good news. With the Russians' attention diverted from the war, any support on the western front would be helpful.

"An' I don't suppose it'll be too long now before the Ford Motor Company'll start makin' armoured vehicles," I said, passing the newspaper across the kitchen table to my wife.

We had finished our tea, our sweet bowls scraped clean; once again Ada had made a rice pudding, such was the lack of fresh fruit and pastries in the shops. The pudding was somewhat enlivened by a dollop of strawberry jam, courtesy of my mother-in-law who had made the preserve in bulk quantities the previous summer at a time when sugar was not so scarce.

For a little while at least, preparing the meal had taken my wife's mind off the tribulations of St Hilda's choir and their attempts to show a harmonious face to the world in their Easter performance of *The Crucifixion*. Stainer's oratorio was the ambitious choice of Mr Tetlow, who was determined to stretch the talents of his singers. He had decided weeks ago that no matter how generous Ada had been with her time on the piano, he needed an organist to accompany all of the rehearsals. Mrs Pailthorpe, the regular church organist had her nose put out of joint (she was admittedly a fairly limited musician) when he announced he was engaging a fellow he knew from a church in Fallowfield. I had heard all the grumbles over recent weeks, and now it was coming to a head. *Poor Mrs Pailthorpe! He treated her very brusquely, you know. Mind you, I think most of the choir were secretly glad to see the back of her. She can barely manage 'All Things Bright and Beautiful'.* Ada had since assumed her place in the row of mezzo-sopranos, constantly prodded by Mr Tetlow to reach the higher registers. *He bullies us into overreaching, he thinks we're all professionals. Mrs Windybank, you know, the lady at the post office on Stretford Road, she was giving her all last night in 'God So Loved the World', but he demanded more. More volume. The poor woman's had a terrible cold all week and she just broke down in tears.*

I had been told more than once by my wife that the majority of the choir had thought from the start that *The Crucifixion* was a poor choice for St Hilda's. They had made a worthy attempt two years earlier at Maunder's *Olivet to Calgary*, and the preference was for another stab at that much-loved and more accessible cantata. Mr Tetlow had overruled them in no uncertain terms; the Stainer was a favourite of his late mother's. From a technical point of view, it included hymns for congregational participation which Ada considered a mistake. *The poor souls of St Hilda's won't be familiar with the likes of the Mystery hymns. There's 'The Divine Humiliation' for a start, and then 'The Intercession'.* It was at this point that my interest might begin to sag. *They'll be mumbling along, completely out of tune, knocking the choir right out of our stride. It'll be a mess, I guarantee. And there's a bass solo halfway through, a lovely piece, I admit, but, well, old Mr Etchells, he's floundering with it, poor man. He's very willing, Tetlow does encourage him – see how he treats the men differently – but I just don't think he's got the lungs anymore.*

I stood up, collected the bowls and carried them over to the sink. Ada was reading an article about the involvement of the Americans.

Meanwhile, the thought of Daniel Harrop in uniform was one that recurred. I had read about the landships, referred to more commonly as tanks, and how they were viewed as a tactical trump card. The belief was that they could provide the Allies with a genuine advantage in the land war, breaking the stalemate. In what was described by one journalist as a "race in the development of the technology", Britain was a good way ahead of the Germans and our army had already employed tanks – with limited success, it must be said – along the Somme. The French too had started production. Smashing through enemy lines in armoured gunships – it's the future.

"So Danny will have gone and joined up for no reason, after all," said Ada, shaking her head.

"Well, yes an' no," I answered. "I don't expect he'll see it like that. Once he's got into his uniform an' got his hands dirty, fittin' up tanks an' such, he'll be in his element, an' no mistake."

"But not as safe as if he'd stayed at Trafford Park."

"Happen not. But there was more to it than that."

"What do you mean, Charlie?"

"I dunno. I just got the sense that he wanted – needed – summat more in his life than a factory job in Salford. I saw it in his eyes. Call it excitement, a thrill. Or a sort of escape."

3

TREE ON THE RIDGE

Day by day each solemn dusk I spy you:
My lonely tree, black and stark and silent on the ridge.
Rigid limbs as ripped and racked as lightning-struck,
Bereft, you stand between us, looming from the smoke:
A silhouette of splintering against the dreamy sky.
No leaves, no telling what a tree you are (or were),
What fruit or blossom you once had borne,
What memories of shade or shelter yet you could evoke.

Poison, not the frigid season, stole your sap (for it is June)
And bombs that rent the earth about your roots.
A death dragged out or strangled hibernation?
Will days return when canopies of sparkling foliation
Cast shadows on our smiling girls and boys
In pastel-coloured shirts and shiny summer boots?

AK

The day began inauspiciously with a serious accident at the busy junction of Chester Road and Empress Street. I cannot claim to have been a witness of the event but I arrived moments later in time to see the aftermath. Nobody could blame the weather conditions, as the morning was bright and dry. From what I guessed, and as it was quickly explained, a fellow driving north rather too fast in a motor car failed to spot a child running out of the side street and straight into the traffic. At the last second the driver swerved to avoid the boy, struck him in spite of that, and at the same time found himself in the middle of the road with a beer truck bearing down on him. The inevitable collision destroyed the front of the car, and when I reached the scene, with scores of other folk on their way to work, the driver was being pulled out of the wreckage by a couple of labourers.

People were shrieking, calling for help, steam was shooting from the crumpled bonnet and the engine of the truck throbbed impatiently. The unfortunate motorist was still conscious but was bleeding from the head. Somebody who said they worked at the hospital appeared and took temporary charge. The driver of the truck was quite unscathed but his vehicle was buckled on one side. He stood observing the scene, cap askance, scratching his forehead. Someone shouted that the barrels on his waggon had broken loose and one had rolled into the road. A policeman arrived and began giving orders to clear the area. A woman called out *Where's that young lad gone?* but no-one could say. He had disappeared, probably already scarpering up City Road with a bruised shoulder, hoping to get to school before the bell.

I arrived at Cornbrook Road later than usual as a result of the commotion. The first-floor staff were already largely at their desks, a few fussing in the corner around the big teapot. I made my presence known and was greeted with the customary salutations. As I passed Mr Dewsbury's space I noticed the man was slumped forward with his head in his hands.

171

"Mr Dewsbury," I said, stopping in my tracks. "Are you alright? Are you feeling poorly?"

The man looked up. He appeared paler than usual and he was trembling slightly.

"I'm very well, Mr Knott, sir. I'm sorry, I had a bit of bad news last night and, well, I'm still rather upset." He sat up straight and took a deep breath. "But don't worry, Mr Knott, Master Crompton's just fetching me a cup of tea and a digestive biscuit and I'll be right as rain in a minute."

At that moment the young trainee arrived at the desk carefully carrying a cup and saucer. He smiled at me and placed the drink before his mentor.

"I'll be fine, Mr Knott," insisted Mr Dewsbury. He tapped the top of a pile of documents at his elbow. "You see these insurance papers? I'll have them updated, annotated and filed away before you've read your newspaper headlines, sir."

I smiled, left him to his tea and strode into my office.

Almost immediately Ethel appeared. I mentioned the accident by Empress Street and she agreed that it had become a dangerous corner with all the motorised traffic toing and froing these days. *Would I like a pot of tea now or in half an hour as usual? The paper's not in yet, Mr Knott, but I'll fetch you your mail when you've settled.*

About five minutes later, there was a gentle tap on my door and quite unexpectedly Master Crompton was standing at the threshold with an expression of concern on his whiskerless face.

"Excuse me, Mr Knott, sir…"

"Yes? Come in, Master Crompton, what's to do? You look

like you've lost your wallet."

"It's Mr Dewsbury, sir." He coughed to clear his throat, then continued in a quiet voice: "He's had some bad news, sir."

"Yes, he told me so himself not ten minutes ago. Is he poorly? Does he want to go home?"

"He's already gone, Mr Knott. I'm here to offer his apologies. I think he's been cryin', sir. Just quietly sobbin' to himself. It's seeing the desk, I think, sir. In fact, I'm sure of it. The empty chair an' the empty desk."

"Th'empty desk?"

"Mr South's desk. His friend Mr South. He said I could tell you all of it. You'd understand. He got word last night from Mr South's mother that her son had been killed in action. He was at the front, wasn't he? A place called Arras. There was a raid on the enemy lines. The poor man was hit. I never met him, of course, but I know Mr Dewsbury was very fond of him. They were very close pals, he did tell me. Poor Mr Dewsbury, sir, he's in a very sorry state."

It took a moment for the boy's words to sink in. My blood had chilled.

I asked him to go and fetch Ethel. A card of condolence to the desperate Mrs South was the very least that was called for.

It was not so unusual for a business letter to arrive at my office from the United States but the one that Ethel had placed on top of this morning's pile of mail looked a little out of the ordinary. It came in a pale grey envelope and the unwieldy name, *Phoenix (POM), formerly Booth & Byrne*, and address

173

of our company had been printed on a square of paper glued to conceal a previous destination. On the reverse, I saw that the sender was a woman: Mrs Frieda McGaw of New York City.

I placed my cigarette in the ashtray, sliced open the envelope and removed the contents. I was holding a folded sheet of writing paper and a smaller, yellowed envelope. The page was filled with immaculate, feminine handwriting which I read with growing curiosity:

Dear Mr Knott,

I do hope this correspondence finds you in good health, if indeed it does ever find you at all. You will notice that I have directed it to you care of the Manchester Ship Canal Company as that is the only address I have for you.

You will please find enclosed a letter written to you over twenty years ago by my late father, Mr Isaac Slater of Brooklyn, New York. He passed away in 1896 at the age of seventy-seven years. He had lived in the United States for more than half his lifetime, having spent his earlier years in Hyde, Cheshire, England, where you may have been acquainted with him. He loved to talk of tramping around a place called Werneth Low. He enjoyed a happy life here in New York. He met my mother Lucy and they had a good marriage, I do believe. My grandfather, who was in the clothing business, found him a job in a warehouse and he became the manager of a company depot on the waterfront.

I do apologise if all of this seems irrelevant. You will find his letter to you infinitely more interesting, I am sure. For it is this I am sending to you: a letter he wrote shortly before his death and which, for whatever the reason, he did not post.

My mother died this winter past. She was almost ninety. I have since taken it upon myself to sort through my parents' possessions before I should aim to sell their house. I discovered this letter addressed to England: sealed, stamped and ready to mail. I cannot imagine why he decided not to. Perhaps you will see for yourself. Of course, it remains unopened. The news in it, at least twenty years out of date, is, I dare say, as stale as the fashions from the old century. Nevertheless, I thought it right that you should have it.

I send you my best regards, and let us hope that this dreadful war is soon at an end.

Yours most sincerely,

Frieda McGaw (née Slater)

On the yellowed envelope enclosing the second letter, my name and the address of the Ship Canal Company were clumsily written in sloping capitals. The hand of Isaac Slater? I tried to picture his face but it was impossible. I knew practically nothing about the man. I very vaguely recalled my Uncle James mentioning him to my mother a time or two, but I cannot say he ever spoke of him to me. Most intrigued, and eager to discover why a stranger should choose to write to me – and then abandon his plan – I opened the envelope and unfolded the single sheet of notepaper that it had protected for so many years. It was dated the third of September 1896.

Dear Charles, I read, and was immediately surprised by the writer's informality.

I hope a letter from me does not alarm you. My name is Isaac Slater. You will see that I am an emigrant, living in America.

I am originly from Gee Cross, Hyde, and was a friend of your relative James Shore for many years. Since we were children in fact. We grew up together in distant times.

There were spelling mistakes here and there but I read on undeterred. Who was I to criticise a poorly educated man?

But that's enough about me. I rite with a message concerning my late brother, Joseph. Being only a year younger than me he too knew James, or Jamie as we always called him as pals. Joseph worked with him at the mill down Apethorn Lane which you will know.

I kept in touch with my brother on and off. It seems he had a falling out with Jamie a long time ago. I was informed that Joseph died last winter. Shortly before he died he rote to me a letter explaining the reeson for the dispute. As you know, none of us are Catholics but it was as if he was making a confession. It concerns your mother, Charles, your mother Elizabeth, who we were all so fond of as a lively young girl. It also concerns your father too.

Somehow the next sentence required no reading. Before I even saw the words, they were burned into my consciousness like the mark of a branding iron:

My brother Joseph was your father.

I turned the page over and devoured the rest:

He rote to me of no circumstances. Neither did he rite of love. Perhaps it was an accident, a reckless moment, a loss of control. But believe you me, Charles, your father was my brother. What concerns me, I suppose, is that he never told you. Nobody told you, it seems. Not Jamie, not even your mother. Such was the shame, the gilt. I know that Joseph carried the gilt to his grave, but I beg you to forgive him, forgive them both.

I realised I was trembling. I took a deep breath, held the page more tightly and read until I reached the very end:

I feel you have a right to know and now that he has passed on, you should let him rest in peace. I was told there is a new cemetry on Hyde Lane and I have made arrangements for him to be buryed there.

Should you wish to confront Elizabeth, then that too is your right, Charles, but I would countenance against it. She is a good woman, a good mother. She did her best. It saddens me to admit that I do not even know if she still walks this earth with us.

Let bygones be bygones, my friend. I hesitate to call you my nephew for I am but an old stranger, I do reelise that. Please be assured, however, that my thoughts and prayers are with you.

I wish you a long and prosprous life.

Isaac Slater

It was all I could do to let the page fall to the desk.

I must have sat silently staring into the middle distance for I do not know how long, my mind spinning, my memory racing back and forth like a shuttle on a loom. Unable to picture either Joseph Slater or his brother Isaac, I tried instead to conjure up an image of my mother. No matter how much I wanted, it was impossible to see her as a young mother, the woman who had told me my father had been killed in an engineering accident miles from home. I could only see her as an old woman, a widow worn out by mill work and disappointment. But Elizabeth was no widow: she was a disheartened spinster with two children unbaptised.

I had no reason to believe that Isaac Slater's story was

untrue. He had not even attempted to protect his brother's reputation or to justify his cowardice. And I saw that it was also cowardice, or shame or guilt or all of it, that had formed the callus of my mother's lie. I remembered that I was a child when the lie was first told to me, a four- or five-year-old. At that age I had understood nothing of *loss of control*, of moments of passion, of possession. There was only one reason why she had kept away from him afterwards, and why he had kept his distance from me. Had he bullied her, coerced her so brutally? Could he have actually raped her? The lie had been told to protect me, of course. I remembered being sad that my father had been blown to pieces in a black powder explosion up in the hills, but I got over it without resentment, without lasting anger. I had never known him. Ralph, had she called him? Of course, she had. I had never forgotten the name. She had whispered it to me, with a catch in her voice: *Ralph* – it had sounded like *wolf*. But he was never more than a ghost.

I remembered to breathe. My cigarette had burned out, a neat roll of ash fallen into the bowl.

It was all such a long time ago. Joseph Slater. One little detail about him had always stuck in my mind. On my first day as a menial in the boiler house, James told me that Slater had lost two of his fingers in his first week's work as a ten-year-old piecer at Apethorn Mill. For the rest of his life his hand must have looked more like a claw. He had been not much younger than I was at the time, a daft boy skylarking behind the rattling frames in the spinning room. It was a cautionary tale: respect the machinery.

I was startled by the telephone ringing. A fellow from the CWS (was it Brocklebank?) wanted to amend an order for hold space on the next ship due to leave Cadiz. I told him, no doubt too abruptly, that I would have to locate the paperwork and ring him back later in the day.

I wondered if I should show Ada the letters from Brooklyn. I questioned if it would serve any purpose. She knew the story of Ralph the navvy, as did Alfred. They had assumed that truth with as much equanimity as I had done. My son was very young when his grandmother Elizabeth had died. The whole saga was a small part of the lives of a distant generation. It would make no difference to him at all to know the new truth.

I asked myself about my sister Mary. What had she been told? She too had never known *her* father: a different man, a travelling man who worked on the canals, we were both led to believe. When I was born Mary was already six years old – old enough to understand that my father was absent. I decided that she could not have been given the same explanation as me; she would have known that tales of marriage to a man called Ralph were untrue. Whatever she was told, she had kept it to herself all her life.

James Shore knew everything, of course. He must have confronted Slater at some point. But he told me nothing. It was a matter for their generation, not ours.

And what of Walter Rowbotham? He had been a great friend of James' at the end, a sharer of stories, a confidant indeed. So had Walter known about Slater? Had he deliberately kept those facts from me throughout our own friendship? Had he been sworn to secrecy? It had sometimes struck me as odd that Walter had not set down elements of James' extraordinary life in writing. He loved to write. He had written a lengthy manuscript – he even described it to me as an attempt at a novel – detailing his love of Hyde Football Club, which I was encouraged to read. James' story, of which I knew a large part – his involvement with the Hyde Chartists, the riots in the mills, the time spent in prison and so on – would also have made an interesting narrative, I am sure. I have no doubt that anything Walter may have begun along those lines was never completed. He would have shown me, I am certain of it, and I never saw such a manuscript.

4

I had no opportunity to question my sister Mary on the subject of my father's identity. Less than a week after I received the letter from Frieda McGaw, another piece of mail arrived quite out of the blue, this time at Isabella Street. An envelope bearing the postmark Huddersfield, West Yorkshire, contained a card upon which was presented the news that my sister had recently passed away. In no more than three short sentences her husband, a gentleman named Abraham Wright, explained that the cause of death was pneumonia, the funeral had already taken place at a church in Slaithwaite, and I was invited to attend a memorial service which had been arranged at Hyde Chapel on a date in July.

The note had, I confess, little effect on me. Perhaps I took a moment to reflect on my own mortality, but the truth of it was that the loss of my sister would have no impact on my life. We had never been close siblings, and half-siblings at best. As I child I can remember her taking me up the Gerrards to the chapel school in Gee Cross: always reluctantly, always grumbling. Although she must have been only eleven or twelve, she was already working some hours at the mill and she liked the company of the older girls. There was nothing to bind us beyond our mother who was forever short of energy, short of money, even short of love. Mary resented me, there is no doubt about that. Later on, when the young lads of the village showed an interest in her, she became flirtatious; I could describe her as promiscuous once I was old enough to understand what that word meant.

Following our mother's death, she left Hyde and found weaving work in mills in neighbouring towns. I saw her very rarely. There were times when she appeared at my door – she even traced me to Salford – asking me to lend her money. Just as she moved from one job to the next, from one town to another, so she shifted her affections between men. Finally, she found a man who would marry her: an apothecary in Ashton-under-Lyne, Abraham Wright, a fellow almost twenty years her senior. I was not invited to the wedding. I guessed at the time that she had married him more for survival than for love, for she was already ailing. Their union produced no children: I had neither nephew nor niece. At some point they moved to Yorkshire and I saw even less of her: even cards at Christmastime were irregular.

For all of that, my one abiding memory of my sister was her crooked smile and, behind it, a mouthful of bad teeth. And now Mary was gone for good. I read the card again and made a note of the date. It was the least I could do to say a proper farewell, I supposed.

I had no idea what to expect on the afternoon of the service. That I was the only man inside the chapel, save for the minister, was a surprise, but I was one of fewer than ten people inside the space which was overwhelmingly too large for such a meagre congregation. It was a gloomy day, in keeping with the solemn occasion. The arrangements had been made by some of Mary's friends from the village, friends from her younger years who still lived locally. I recognised one or two and we had cordial words. I was introduced more than once as Mary's little brother. A lay preacher led a short service of remembrance and one of the ladies gave a touching eulogy. There was no sign of the Reverend Dowson.

I say I was the only man present, but that is not strictly accurate. Halfway through the proceedings, a tall man with a walking stick joined us, discreetly introducing himself as Abraham Wright, Mary's widower. A healthy complexion, lustrous white hair and a robust beard belied his age, which I estimated to be close to eighty. He had journeyed over the Pennines with a young woman, a great-niece, on a train to Stalybridge which had been delayed. Thence they had found a taxicab to bring them the five miles to Gee Cross.

Mary's friends had arranged refreshments to be served at the Grapes Inn at the top of the village. We had cheese sandwiches and buttered currant loaf and here the atmosphere became lighter, gayer, especially when Mr Wright announced he would like to pay for all the drinks consumed by our party. As we split into smaller groupings, amusing tales were retold by the women of escapades involving Mary – incidents which had passed me by but which Mr Wright was at least in part familiar with. The man had his own anecdotes involving a cheerful, generous and loving companion: descriptions of my sister which I struggled to recognise.

At around six o'clock groups of drinkers began to arrive to quench their thirst after a day's labour. One or two of the faces seemed familiar but I remembered that it was thirty years since I had lived in this place. Sitting with the three or four of Mary's friends who remained – Mr Wright and his great niece had left us an hour or so earlier – I was ignored by every visitor to the bar apart from one: a bald-headed fellow who had grown a substantial paunch since I had last laid eyes upon him. It was Robert Howarth, the greengrocer's son, a teammate of mine in numerous cricket matches once upon a time. He entered the room alone, removed his cap and spotted me straight away.

"Is that you, Charlie Knott?" he asked, his voice filling the space between us. The women looked up from their glasses.

"You know him, Charlie?" one of them enquired.

"Course he does," answered Howarth on my behalf. "An' I know *him*, an' all. Come over here, my friend, an' let me shake you by the hand. How long's it been?"

I stood up and let him embrace me like a lost brother, which in itself was somewhat incongruous: we were never the best of friends, rather two lads from the same village that sport had happened to throw together.

"Well, I was up here for Walter's funeral," I said. "What's that? About six year ago. An' then today, it was our Mary's."

"Well, any road, it's grand to see you, old fella," said Howarth, fishing out some coins from his pocket. "I'll buy you a beer, o' course. You're lookin' well. Still livin' in Manchester, is it?"

"Salford, it is, really," I said. "Aye, we're very settled."

A minute or two later, with a glass of ale in each hand, he led me over to a small table by the empty fireplace. I offered him a cigarette and for a moment we smoked together like a pair of old comrades. He seemed to have trouble quelling his grin. I never recalled him being quite so genial; he must have had a most rewarding day behind the counter of his shop.

"I've expanded the business, Charlie," he was saying. "You remember, the grocery business. You've probably not 'ad time to notice it. I bought the premises next door – doubled the floor space. Mind you, it's not the best time to be in business, as you must know. The war's hit folk's wallets, an' no mistake. Nobody's spendin' like they used to. An' oftentimes we can't even fill our shelves in any case. You know, there's certain

184

commodities that're scarce. We do alright with farm produce, o' course, but imported goods, forget it, Charlie. This damn war, it needs finishin'. The poison that is politics, eh?"

He took a long gulp of his beer, washing away the slurry of words, making room for more:

"You still with the Canal Company, is that right? An' 'ow's the wife? I've forgotten 'er name, I confess, if I ever knew it, o' course. But I did 'ear you were wed. Did you ever 'ave any children? You still playin' a bit o' cricket, by the way? Terrorisin' batsmen with your fast uns like you used to for the Chapel?"

I was unsure in which order he wished me to answer his questions. In fairness to the man, he did seem genuinely interested. His marriage to Louisa Thornley, regarded at the time as the most beautiful woman in Gee Cross, was thriving, he said, and had produced three daughters, now all in their twenties. The eldest, Cecilia, herself married and living in Bredbury, had recently provided them with a granddaughter. Louisa still found time to paint, to ride, and had read every novel that the fellow Dickens had ever written:

"There's some bloody big books he's done, an' all. She's a fanatic, she really is!"

I mentioned Alfred, his curtailed career as a journalist and his current predicament in northern France.

"I 'onestly feel blessed to 'ave 'ad daughters, Charlie," he said, rising from his seat to buy another round of drinks. "Our Cecilia's fella's a lucky beggar. He's a teacher. Needed on the home front, as they say. I dunna envy you the worry of 'avin' a lad in the trenches. You must 'ave sleepless nights, you an' Edie."

"Ada."

"Sorry, Charlie. Ada. Ada, o' course. Any road, you must 'ave sleepless nights, pair o' you."

"We have to hope for the best, Robbie. An' Ada's a great one for prayer."

"Prayer? Well, that's quite another matter. Hm. Same again?"

"Aye, thanks. But let me pay this time."

"Put your money away, pal. You're me guest. I've 'ad an excellent day today. I feel like celebratin'."

"Oh, aye?"

"I've 'ad my eye on a little grocery business up Godley that's been up for sale. I put in an offer a fortnight ago an' got word today it's been accepted."

"Very good. Congratulations."

"Indeed, Charlie. Indeed. It's not a good time to sell, you know, with the war on an' all. But a very good time to buy," he added, tapping the side of his nose with a stubby forefinger. "An' so, the empire grows! You fancy a whisky, do you, while I'm gettin' 'em in?"

When Howarth finally remembered he had a home to go to with his tea waiting for him on the table, I too decided it was time to take my leave. The women I had arrived with had long since departed. I cannot remember the time it was but the sun had been scarce all day and an early dusk was falling. I do recall feeling slightly drunk, and at the same time grateful that my walk down Hyde to the tramway terminus was a most familiar one.

The air was still, cooling a little, as I strode down Hyde Lane, past the Big Tree, the new streetlamps popping on intermittently. It took me little more than ten minutes to come upon the entrance to the wide, sloping field that had been turned into a municipal cemetery some time around the turn of the century. Nowadays there was a driveway lit by a pair of lamps, a low brick wall and wrought-iron gates, all of which I had never seen before. There was not a living soul about. Curiosity overcame me and I made my approach. Beyond the gates I could see in silhouette row upon row of gravestones, crosses and statuettes and raised squares of earth beneath dark banks of shrubs and young trees.

I lifted the heavy latch on the gate and discovered it to be unlocked. I slid in between the space like the stealthiest of burglars and found myself passing a stone-built lodge and a water pump. Within twenty yards I was already among the graves. The light had all but faded but I made up my mind to search as best I could and allowed myself five minutes. If I failed to find it then I would leave; darkness would defeat me in the end. Of course I knew exactly what I was looking for. I knew the moment I realised that the cemetery would be on my way home. The well-established New Yorker Isaac Slater, son-in-law of a wealthy Brooklyn trader, had "made arrangements for him to be buryed" in this place. *Him* being my father, the furtive Joseph, the man who had denied me all his adult life. More of a burglar than I would ever be. The man for whom I was an embarrassment, a source of shame, a dirty secret.

I studied the inscriptions on the first row of headstones and, disappointed, quickly moved along the lines. Here I was now, stooping to read carved words, lighting a match, then another, then striking a third, stumbling in the dark, desperate to find him before the flame burned out. And suddenly I did find it, and stopped as if frozen in my tracks: a large, flat slab of what looked like marble. I struck another match. There was no flamboyant decoration, no winged cherub in stone. Below a simple design of a laurel wreath were carved the words: *Rest In Peace – Joseph Edmund Slater 1821-1895 – Loving Son and Brother*. There were no flowers laid at its foot, not even a neglected old vase. I stared at the words for a moment until my match flickered out. I realised I was breathing heavily. Feeling a discomforting pressure on my bladder, I did not hesitate to unbutton my breeches. I relieved myself there and then in the thickening gloom, letting my stream of urine rain down on his headstone, listening to the splash of it, watching the faint wisps of steam rising from the shadows. I left the scene quickly but felt no shame. After all, wasn't this the sort of thing that bastards are expected to do?

5

WOLF PATROL

Behind the mist's soft veil he skulks and prowls,
The vampire of the forest, the stalker in the wood.
Fresh mud on his paws, dried blood upon his jowls,
He knows this mound,
This hunting ground,
More closely than a sniper ever could.

Wolf waits and wanders, sniffing at the evening air:
The smoke, the dust, the smell of autumn drift mean naught.
The stench of man, though, a solitary, will draw him from his
lair.
The shadows of the forest edge,
The greasy ledge:
He lurks, and spies what providence has brought.

A shivering man in a bombed-out hole,
Rifle pointing skywards, hands and ears wrapped tight against
the chill.
Eyes only on the foe, he has no sight nor sound of wolf patrol.
The beast springs out,
A snarling snout
And jaws wide open for the kill.

AK

It took a little time for his mother and me to accustom ourselves to seeing our Alfred with cropped hair and a dark moustache. We both studied him in our own ways as he sat at the kitchen table carefully chipping the top off a boiled egg or standing alone at the back of the house with a cigarette between his fingers and his mind in some faraway place.

It was late summer, it had been eighteen months since he left us, and for a brief time he had been returned to us for home leave: a respite from the fields of war, some fleeting home comforts and the warm embrace of a familiar and cherished place. Of his adventures in France he told us fragments, embellishing what he had written about in his letters. He spoke of new friendships, some cut short, he spoke of his frustration with a number of his commanding officers, of the boredom of endless, dreary days where nothing much happened beyond aimless artillery strikes back and forth. He told us of the inconsistency of the food the troops were given, the relief of the reserve trenches and precious time spent in Abbéville, away from the lines. With a smile on his face he mentioned the songs he had learned, the games he had played, the time he could enjoy with lads from all parts of Britain and some from lands he had hardly heard of.

Ada was relieved to hear that he was not in the firing line so much. I knew, and I suppose that in her heart she did too, that there was a great deal he had not said. There were pictures in his head too cruel, too harrowing to be described to his mother over a cup of tea and a scone. We were spared the worst, and I dare say the worst *had* been visited upon our son more often than either of us wanted to think about.

Even when I found myself alone with Alfred, I refrained from asking questions about the dangers of the combat, the near misses, the comrades he had lost. If he wanted to broach these subjects, I thought, then he would. But so far, he never did.

He was pleased to be home, of course. His smile, even his laugh, was still intact, as was his appetite for bacon and sausages and warm meat pies, but his demeanour was generally more serious than before. As for his health, we found him robust and a shade more muscular. Where the experience had left its mark was in the boy's face. His eyes, once so bright and mischievous, had lost their sparkle. Beneath them a hint of greyness pouched on his cheekbones. In spite of the season, his complexion was sallow. His hands bore scratches at the knuckles, his fingernails were split and browned. And both his parents, in separate moments, noticed how yellow his teeth had become, stained by endless tea and tobacco.

Sometimes, in response to an apparently trivial question from either one of us, Alfred remained silent and wandered away with a solemn expression on his face as if he had not heard our words at all. He appeared to be interested in our lives merely up to a point. Indeed, he spent periods of time away from Isabella Street, disappearing without warning, only to reappear with an enthusiastic report of where he had been and what he had seen. One day he wandered into the tap room of the Red Rose, had bumped into one of his old schoolteachers and had what he called "a lovely chat". Another time he sat on a wall outside the school on Powell Street and watched as the children bustled out of the gates and homewards when the bell was rung. And one afternoon he had walked the mile to Salford Docks and stared at the large cargo ships moored there, their exotic names taking his mind on journeys a long, long way beyond England, beyond Europe. Some years ago, I had played the same game myself: a game of imagination, where just a name – Marseille, New York, Bombay – was enough to ignite thoughts of an adventure. Thoughts, but no actions. As Alfred listed the vessels to me upon his return, I nodded encouragingly; having been over to the Trafford Road side on business quite recently myself, I knew every one of the ships he mentioned.

For many months the port of Liverpool had reduced its capacity for trading ships out of necessity, for much of its dockside space was turned over to repair work. More and more vessels were arriving in a poor state, generally damaged by German submarines, and of those that had safely crossed the Atlantic, a larger proportion were redirected to Manchester at that time. And so it was that Alfred had spotted ships that had arrived from ports in the Americas, North and South: from New York and Charleston, from Buenos Aires and Paramaribo. One of the ships, *San Cristobel*, was on our books and had sailed from Argentina carrying beef, stopping on her way in Havana to load up with sugar. I had met her captain only a day or two earlier: he was a wiry man, Ramirez, a Cuban, with sun-baked skin like tanned leather, and he spoke English with an almost impenetrable accent. He was full of praise for the crew of the Royal Navy frigate which had escorted them through dangerous waters as far as the Irish Channel. As we parted, he gifted me a small wooden box which contained half a dozen plump cigars: a most generous gesture. I promised him I would start smoking them the day the war was over.

On another day, shortly before he was due to leave us, Alfred walked the two miles to Chorlton-cum-Hardy to visit his grandmother. The last time he had seen her his grandfather had been at her side.

"She's become a sad old woman," I heard him saying upon his return.

He was in the kitchen with his mother, both of them facing the stove where Ada was gently frying an onion and some sliced potatoes in the skillet. Neither of them had heard me appear. I stood and watched them from the doorway. Ada nodded and gave him a smile of resignation.

"She's so diminished," the lad went on. "It's so sad, mother. It's not fair, is it? Why can we not turn back time?"

I noticed my wife take his hand in hers and squeeze it softly. He leaned towards her and kissed her forehead so tenderly. I had to back out of the room for fear of them seeing the tears falling from my eyes.

One afternoon, on the Saturday of his leave as I recall, I suggested to Alfred that we walk over to Hullard Park together for a game of bowls. It was something we had enjoyed now and again when he was still a schoolboy. I was gratified that he accepted the idea without hesitation. Ada insisted we had tea first: she had managed to find some oranges on the market and had made a marmalade cake for us all, but more especially for her son.

The little booth by the bowling green was still open as we arrived, and the old fellow sitting in its shadows was prepared to let us have a set of bowls each for forty-five minutes before he closed up for the evening. The lawn was empty save for a trio of young women who were giggling and squealing as, in turn, they made laughable efforts to roll their bowls close to the jack. I imagined that each one of them might have a boyfriend or a young husband they were missing, sent from these Salford streets to shoot at Germans across some foreign field. On noticing Alfred, they nudged each other and for a minute or two endeavoured to raise their game, hoping to impress him with their accuracy. If my son was aware of their attention he did not show it, and the women grew tired of concentrating, quickly returning to their frivolity and slap-dash interpretation of the rules.

Meanwhile our own game began and it was clear that we were evenly matched: my days of superiority had long since passed. Alfred had the eyes, the loose limbs, the very feel for the sport, landing his bowls close to their target with maddening consistency. I had to be at my best to keep pace with his score. Presently the women left the arena with some fanfare but Alfred had eyes only on his victory, which was becoming more inevitable with every end. Afterwards we found a bench to sit on and smoked cigarettes.

"You played very well, Alfred," I said through gritted teeth, for my reputation as a sportsman with a most competitive nature had never waned.

"We play a lot of bowls over there," he said. "You know, in France."

"Really?"

"Don't be daft, Father," he answered, breaking into a broad grin. "You think they have bowling greens dotted around, in between the trenches?"

I felt a little foolish, unused to his teasing.

"If only," he went on, staring out across the empty lawn which was glowing in the early evening sunlight. "The only sport I play is football. We have matches when we're away from the front, resting up. One regiment against another, or happen a game against the Frenchies."

"No cricket, then?"

"Not really. I know it pains you to hear it but I was never one for cricket much anyway."

I said nothing, took a pull on my cigarette.

"I think I've found my calling, though," he was saying. "As an amateur sportsman, I mean. It's as a goalkeeper. I'm always picked as a goalie and they say I'm a good one. It suits me, I think. When we come back for good, after the war is won, I shall look for a team in Manchester to play with. I've made my mind up."

A little flock of sparrows, pecking at the footpath on the far side of the lawn, suddenly fluttered into the air as a black cat sprang out from the depths of a hedge. We laughed as one, seeing the incident and the sullen reaction of the animal. My cigarette had burned out and I made to get up.

"Shall we have a drink?" I said. "Loser pays so it'll be my pleasure to treat my son to a beer at the Full Tun."

"Sorry, Father," came the reply. "I've got to be on my way now. I think I'm already late."

"Late? Late for what?"

"I'm meeting some of the Gaiety crowd in town."

"Are you?"

"I said."

"I din't know."

"I said. It must have been Mother I told. Sorry. You don't mind, do you?"

I leaned back on to the slats of the bench.

"No. No, you go off an' catch up with your friends."

He flicked his cigarette end to the ground and squashed it with the heel of his boot.

"You always tell your mother more than me," I said.

"Do I?"

"I believe so. Happen that's what sons do. It's what I did. Mind you, I'd no father to speak to, did I?"

"There's plenty I've not said to her."

I looked across to catch his eye.

"Lately," he added. "Stuff I've not put in my letters. Stuff I could have told you both these last few days."

"About the fightin'?"

"About what it's like being scared shitless day after day, night after night, waiting for the bombs to land, the bullets to rattle over, the gas clouds to fall. And that's when you're still in your shelter, under cover, supposedly safe."

I looked away, let him say as much or as little as he wished. The black cat had disappeared. The sparrows were back, beaks scratching at the ground.

"Then the order'll come," he continued slowly, softly. "An order from some know-nowt officer to mount a charge. Take hold of a ridge, push Fritzi out of a farmhouse, even attack their front line. While it's pissing down. Happen in the dark."

He turned to face me, eyes focussed on mine but somehow deadened.

"You can't imagine the terror, Father, the terror of what's to come, what's out there waiting for you. When that bugle calls. Then the horror you find between the lines. The barrage of bullets. Rat-a-tat-tat. Rat-a-tat-tat. Your mates hit, falling wounded into the mud. Or worse. Body parts scattered like litter. It's like hell, or how you might imagine it. Desperate men stumbling through clouds of smoke like they've lost their minds. The screams of the damned rising above the thunder. Balls of fire barrelling across the blackened earth. And it's a lottery who comes back and who doesn't. Whose number comes up. And in the end, it's all for nothing."

He stopped talking. A few people were passing nearby but to us they had become invisible.

"I see death as a wolf," Alfred said suddenly. "I see a stalking wild animal, picking off its prey in some mindless, savage, random way."

I gave him an inquisitive look.

"In my poems. Like a motif," he explained. "I told you I was writing poetry, didn't I?"

"You sent us some examples, Alfred. They're very fine. We kept 'em all."

"There's plenty of time for writing. In between the slaughter."

"Then you must keep writin'. It carries your mind somewhere else, I suppose. An' you have a talent for it, an' no mistake."

Suddenly he stood up. The frown had become a smile.

"That's what the army has taught me," he laughed. "I have talents for writing poems and playing in goal! Look, Father, I'd better be going. They'll be wondering where I am."

"You 'ave a nice time," I said, standing to pat him on the shoulder. Both his mother and I had taken to touching him more than we ever used to, keen to feel the fabric of his clothes, his bristly hair, the warmth of his skin. We knew Alfred was only with us on loan. For a short period of sweet September days we were just borrowing our son, and then we must give him back.

I watched Alfred stride away out of the park, towards Northumberland Road, and out of sight. I might have said "march away", such was his upright gait: that of a soldier, an infantryman. My son, the warrior.

The sun was dipping behind the rooftops of the terraced streets but the air remained warm and placid. One or two people were still about, taking a stroll in the gardens, stopping here and there to admire a tree still in full leaf, a row of rosebushes in late bloom, a bed of sparkling marigolds. I took out another cigarette, lit it and made myself comfortable, alone on the bench. Beyond the faint voices there was barely a sound. I heard the soft whinny of a horse somewhere, then a child squealing in a nearby street. There was the yelp of a dog in the distance, the twittering of the birds, but little else. For a moment the traffic at this edge of the city seemed to have stopped, the great factories not so far away fallen silent hours ago.

Under a ripple of high white cloud, I smoked my cigarette and watched the shadows of the trees creeping across the flat expanse of lawn. To me the city was as far away as Havana, as Paramaribo. As far away as the Western Front. Would that the guns fell silent for this long across those wretched killing fields. And then be silenced for ever.

"Sir? Mister?"

I was startled by a young man in a dark blue jerkin standing over me.

"Mister?" he repeated, his strange voice filled with anxiety. "Please, mister."

"What's to do?" I asked, sitting up to better engage with him.

He was square-built and had short, fair hair and pale blue eyes, somewhat bloodshot.

"It's my friend, sir. He is fallen. Over there."

The fellow pointed to the far side of the park where, hidden behind a high line of bushes, a gentlemen's toilet was to be found. His accent was unusual to me. That he was foreign was clear, but to my ears he was neither French nor Spanish.

"Over there?" I said. "Is he poorly?"

"Poorly?"

"Ill. Is your friend ill?"

"He is drinking, sir. We are both drinking, I must say. But he is drinking too much, I think so."

"Are you Dutch?"

"I am Norwegian, sir. Sailor. I am hoping you are doctor, perhaps."

"I'm not a doctor, but let's see if I can help your friend."

"You are kind, sir. Please. He is fallen. There is blood."

I followed the young man across the park and through the trees, now in shadow, towards the small brick building with a half-opened door painted in bright green. Unsurprisingly the gloomy place housed an unsavoury smell. Once inside,

I found a man doubled over on the damp floor, groaning in the dark, clasping his stomach as if he were about to vomit. I leaned forward to touch his shoulder.

"Sir," I called to him. "What's to do? Where does it hurt? Can you sit up?"

I waited for an answer but instead received a sudden, sharp blow to the back of my head. The Norwegian must have clouted me with a blunt weapon of some kind. Before I could half-turn to confront him, my nose and mouth were covered by a moist rag, held tight over my face: a sweet smell, like roasted nuts, like cut grass, filled my nostrils and made me dizzy, made me faint. I must have fallen to the floor for the next thing I remembered, I was lying belly down on the ground with a cloth stuffed into my mouth and fastened there tight by a strip of knotted cotton. Someone called my name. *Knott.* A voice that echoed. *Knott. Knott.*

I made to stand up but felt nauseous even at the thought.

"Don't try to move," said the same voice, now steadier, sharper in my ears. "It took a while, so it did, Mr Knott, but here we are. We found you in the end."

An Irish voice.

I strained my neck to look up to the face of my tormentor. He was a tall fellow, self-possessed, not drunk at all. His thin face betrayed no emotion. My gaze was drawn to his left hand, which held a butcher's cleaver. And then back to the hand itself: even in the shadows I could see tattooed between the thumb and forefinger the design of a swallow. And suddenly the whole scene took on a brutal inevitability.

Before I knew it, the other man, the so-called Norwegian, was on top of me, weightier than he looked, but the truth of it was I had no strength to fight back. His knees pinned my shoulders to the ground, my head was forced to one side, and with both hands he held my trembling right wrist hard to the floor.

"Open your fist, Mr Knott," ordered the Irishman, crouching so that his bony face was closer to mine. "Spread your fingers."

I refused, knowing all the while that my stubbornness would be futile.

"Please," he insisted, a peculiar note of concern in his voice. "You lose the fingers or you lose the hand." He was kneeling by my side, setting himself. He tapped the edge of the great blade against the concrete floor. "This bastard'll take the wrist in one blow. It's your choice."

I opened my fist, tried to call out something, anything: *Stop! Help! Have mercy!* but the lump of cloth in my mouth prevented all but a deadened, sickly cough. I saw the cleaver hovering an inch above my knuckles. Then the smell again. The roasted nuts. The cut grass. And then the swish and savage slicing of the guillotine.

Much later I was told that I was discovered by the choirmaster of St Hilda's. It appeared that Mr Tetlow was inside the church with his invalid wife and the organist from Fallowfield, discussing some ideas for a concert at the end of the year. All of a sudden, a young blond chap with a foreign accent ran into the building, screaming in broken English that there was a man dying in the toilets on the far side of Hullard Park. By the time Mr Tetlow had asked the musician to keep an eye on his wife, crossed over the road and headed into the park, the stranger had quite disappeared.

It seemed that the assailants had wanted to punish me but not to kill me. It was explained that the chloroform used to immobilise me also had anaesthetic properties. I was found unconscious, slumped in a puddle of my own blood, and my right wrist had been raised and bound to a water pipe. It was in the gutter of the urinal where Mr Tetlow noticed, to his horror, four severed fingers in various stages of their watery journey to the drain hole.

I awoke several hours later, I can now estimate. I was lying in a bed in Salford Infirmary. As I opened my eyes and began to focus, I saw a nurse to my left and my wife Ada to my right, pale of face and with her hands to her cheeks. A searing pain throbbed at my temples and there was an acute stinging sensation welling up and then receding in my right hand, wrapped as it was in yards of bandage and set upon the coverlet like a gift. These physical torments were a part of my existence for days and days.

Much later, once the swelling had finally subsided and the wounds had healed, I was fitted with a glove of soft lamb's skin, beige in colour and close enough to flesh tone to be relatively inconspicuous. It covered my fingerless hand while allowing a neat hole for the thumb – a most useful appendage which I was so generously spared.

The Manchester constabulary were unable to trace my attackers. There was no Norwegian ship in port on the day of the crime, apparently, but nobody necessarily believed that the younger man was actually Norwegian in any case. Two vessels leaving for Dublin later that week were searched. The port police in Liverpool were also put on alert. A detective told me that the pair would probably have split up, gone to ground for a while, and would try to escape by a convoluted route, perhaps by way of Scotland, assuming Ireland was their destination.

The punishment was retribution, of course. I understood that. Murdering Mulloy had not been enough, and certainly not the end of the matter, for their business with Martyn Byrne had been terminally compromised. Quite evidently, I had been traced. It was not difficult to discover, I suppose, that I was a glorified clerk, that the pen was the tool of my trade, that my writing hand was at the very crux of my work. I asked myself how they had known I was right-handed. Had they watched me playing an innocent game of bowls with my son? Had they simply seen me light up a cigarette? I was grateful that my invaluable thumb allowed me to hold a cigarette, however awkwardly, against what remained of my hand. As for gripping a cricket ball, my days of bowling fast ones down a flat wicket were, without warning, over for good.

With regard to my writing, however, those days are not quite at an end. At my work I was granted permission to employ a junior clerk to take dictation whenever I had something important to compose. Master Crompton volunteered to help in the first months of my return to Cornbrook Road; he quickly learned to recognise my almost illegible attempts to make notes and he was willing to transcribe them for me if I wished. In the meantime, I tried to learn how to hold a pencil in my left hand. I could manage a sentence or two but it was the essence of frustration. And so these very words you are following, dear reader, were brought to you from my head and my heart and from my own mouth, assuredly, but not directly from my pen. Every word you have read and every one you will read until the very last was written by Ada. She is the most patient and diligent scribe I could wish for. She also corrects my imprecise spelling and repairs my grammatical inaccuracies. She even tidies up my writing desk if I am of a mind to allow it. Oh, Ada Dooley. In so many ways, and it is no exaggeration to state this, I would be utterly lost without her.

6

I never believed that Alfred would be killed in battle. The worry that something dreadful, something horrific might happen to him gnawed at my heart for month after month, but deep down I never imagined him as one of the fallen, one of the sacrificial lambs. I was sure that he would come back home to us in the end.

In those late months of 1917 it seemed that news from France was ever more sporadic, delayed, rewritten for the purposes of propaganda. We read of fragile advances around the Belgian town of Ypres, and of strategic decisions which were contentious, it was rumoured, even amongst members of the defence staff. Meanwhile the number of casualties was glossed over. It served the establishment's purpose that events in Russia were without doubt a distraction at the time. The uneasy arrangement put in place after the February uprising was swept away with renewed violence in early November. There were widespread mutinies in the Russian army and it was only a matter of time before the country ceased its fighting against Germany entirely. Mr Lenin's Bolsheviks took control of Petrograd, including the Winter Palace, and the Provisional Government fell. Decrees had been made to redistribute land and property among the workers, symbols of the bourgeoisie being targeted with as much venom as those of the aristocracy. I write "*Mr* Lenin" as is our accepted convention, but I do understand that he now prefers the egalitarian title 'Comrade' to be used in his homeland. It was clear that Russia was in the throes of a revolution; there was no other word for what was happening across that vast country. Even from a distance of over one thousand miles, it was exhilarating and frightening in equal measure just to read about it.

Then suddenly we received news of our son.

It was the briefest of notes, wrapped in a grey envelope with a military stamp, and written, whether out of duty or kindness we could not say, by an officer of Alfred's regiment. Alfred had been wounded on the thirtieth of October, he wrote, by enemy fire during an advance on positions close to the Belgian village of Passchendaele. He had been withdrawn to a military hospital. The officer believed that his wounds were no longer an immediate threat to his life.

My heart was thumping as I read the words. I realised I had not let out a breath until I reached the end. Until the sweet phrase *no longer an immediate threat to his life* seeped into my consciousness. Only then, only when a warm rush of relief coursed through my veins, did I pass on the slip of paper to Ada who had stood facing me, drained of colour, she too holding her breath, her hands to her mouth, stifling a shriek of anguish.

Amiens, 10th November 1917

Dearest Mother and Father,

I can imagine you have been worrying about me. Here I am though, sitting up in bed in the hospital in Amiens, writing to you. I am still weak but you can be assured that I will survive this. I will be sent home, they tell me. I am no use to anybody with my wounds.

I can hardly remember what happened to me. Our unit was ordered to punch a hole through Fritzi's lines west of a village called Passiondale. I can't spell it in Belgian. There was smoke and bullets everywhere, shouting and screaming – the usual mix of heroism and blind panic. I was hit with machine-gun fire after less than a minute. You don't see it coming. I remember falling, then I must have passed out. I don't even know if the mission was a success. Luckily I wasn't so far from our lines and I was picked up and dragged over the mud back to the trenches. They patched me up and kept me there for a day before they took me out of the battle.

I'll be alright, believe me. They've taken bullets out of my shoulder and upper arm. Left side, so I can still write, thank God. I lost a lot of blood, they said. I'm bandaged up like a proper invalid. Drugged up to ease the pain. I now know how Father was, losing his fingers. But I'll be alright.

It's a nice hospital but very crowded. The nurses, French of course, are so kind to us.

I will write again when I am stronger.

I hope you are both well in dear old Manchester.

Your loving son,

Alfred

As the year juddered to its close, two more letters arrived from France, and with them, as our son's recovery progressed, so our hopes rose that this year we might share the joy of seeing him at our family table on Christmas Day.

Amiens, 26th November 1917

Dearest Mother and Father,

I received your letter a day or two ago. It was nice to see your lovely handwriting again, Mother. It's good that Father's hand has healed and he's now back at work.

I am glad I could put your minds at rest. I am feeling better already and can sit up for longer than before. I am allowed to walk about a bit, even outside with a greatcoat on. Just for five minutes. It's cold now, winter is here and there's nothing much to see in the garden in any case.

I have found plenty to read. There are books, magazines and sometimes a recent newspaper. Some are in French but I've made friends with a few lads from Ontario (Canada) and they know French. (I can't believe what's happening in Russia. Father, you always said there'd be trouble, didn't you?) The hospital is full of French, Canadians, British, all of us rescued from the battle with bad injuries.

I've begun to get some feeling back in my arm. I can move it around a bit. I'm desperate to scratch at the itches. Nobody can guarantee it'll ever heal properly. It looks like my time as a goalkeeper will have been very short.

They feed us well, better than up on the front line. There's lots of soups, what they call 'potage', like Mother's broth. And 'saucisson', which is a thick spicy sausage they slice and eat cold. It's very tasty. I checked the spelling with Joleon (Canadian). And cheese. We get proper Cheshire cheese. I think it's supplied by the Red Cross. It must be sent over by the waggonload. We even had it a time or two in the trenches, great white slabs to cut up and share. The Frenchies can't be doing with it. They have their Camembert. Deliveries every day, I'm imagining. They share it around. It's lovely cheese, as a matter of fact. Do you remember bringing home a big smelly disc of it from that French ship that time, Father? Before the war? I remember you hated it and even got annoyed when Mother and I said we liked it. We did have a laugh about it, behind your back. Believe me, it's the *future!*

I nearly forgot to mention that I came across a familiar face in here yesterday: your pal Danny Harrop. He was in a bad state but wanted to talk when he recognised me. He's been out here with the tanks – mending them, maintenance and such. I told him they were no good in the craters and pools of mud where we were last year. Neither use nor ornament. He said they did a better job around Cambray where he's been, further south. Took the Germans by surprise on firmer ground. But that's where he'd taken a hit, poor bloke. Out in the fields salvaging at night, he said. His unit was hit by random shelling. Danny got back in but he's lost half his leg. It's a damn cruel place. I'm just glad to be out of it and still in one piece.

Please write back soon. I'll be here a while longer yet. Keep smiling.

All my love,

Alfred

Rouen, 11th December 1917

Dear Mother and Father,

Thank you for your parcel. I ate one of the Eccles cakes each afternoon for as long as they lasted but I shared the toffees with a couple of Canadian pals. We play cards every night and they're teaching me new games. They cheat like mad.

Some of us have been moved to a base hospital in Rouen run by the Army Medical Corps. It's a long way from the fighting. I don't know if this means I'll be home sooner.

I trust you are both in good health. How's the winter in Manchester so far? It's turned very cold here and the nurses tell us it's been snowing. I'm not allowed outside for the time being, which I hate. My shoulder is healing well but my arm's not so good. It throbs with pain and I lose feeling in my left hand now and again. It's some kind of infection, the doctor says, but he'll cure it. A nurse washes the wounds twice a day with disinfectant. I have to be patient. A patient patient! I hope I'll be sent home in time for Christmas. Being in Isabella Street, sitting by Mother's decorated tree, smelling the goose roasting – it would be heaven indeed. Father, you must save me one of your Cuban cigars!

I desperately want to be out of this place. Men wake up in the dead of night weeping and wailing. The smells are disgusting now that they keep the windows shut. When all's said and done, it is a place of suffering.

Danny Harrop was moved here before me. He's in a bed not far from mine. I wander over for a chat now and then and they've found him a wheelchair – they call it a rolling chair! – so he can move about a bit. They operated on his leg. They've amputated it above the knee, so he has a bandaged-up stump of a thigh. It must upset him terribly but he's usually in a cheerful mood. I think I know why.

There's a nurse here, a motherly sort, who he's fallen for. She was dedicated to looking after him after the surgery and she still finds more time for Danny than anyone else, it seems to me. She's called Marie-Anne, he told me. He follows her around the place in his rolling chair when he has the strength. I'm sure he mithers her to death but she doesn't mind. It's quite sweet really. I've seen them whispering and giggling together. She must speak a bit of English because I don't think Danny knows much French, does he?

Yesterday he took me by surprise: he told me he wants to marry her. We had a laugh about it but I think he was delirious with all the drugs they give him. He cannot be serious. For a start, he has a wife at home, doesn't he? He was telling me about the tanks, the Mark Four, they're called, the new ones. We're way ahead of the Germans, so he says. He reckons they could win us the war. He was talking about males and females. Did you know they had boy and girl tanks, Father? You can guess the difference. The female is lighter and armed with just machine guns, whereas the male also has a pair of six-pounder guns. Not one big boy's appendage, but two! Sorry, Mother, this is what it's like surrounded by soldiers all the time.

That's all for now.

It's getting dark anyway. The days are getting shorter but at least I'm warm enough and safe, and the trenches seem a very long way away.

Praying that I'll see you both before long and sending you my love,

Alfred

Part Six
1918

1

Alfred did not return to England in time for Christmas. He was as deflated as we were. A couple of days before his expected repatriation, he wrote from the hospital in Rouen with the news that he had developed septicaemia: a poisoning of the blood caused by an infection in the wounds in his upper arm. The army surgeon was optimistic that the condition was mild but had warned Alfred that the treatment – he had corrosive chemicals and even thermocautery at his disposal – would be unpleasant. This, rather than roast goose and plum pudding, was to be our son's Christmas.

It was some comfort to us to know that amongst the nursing staff and his invalid comrades, our mutual friend Danny Harrop was also a consoling presence. The letter, this time no more than a single page, mentioned a growing friendship between the pair of them. Danny was suffering more than most from night fears. He was being given strong drugs to ease his anxiety but nothing was more effective to calm him than fifteen minutes spent in the company of the French nurse Marie-Anne. He was still reliant on his rolling chair for mobility and although he quickly became fatigued, it seemed he spent as much time as he was allowed in her orbit. He confided in Alfred things he had told nobody before – certainly not me.

Danny is scared about being sent home, that's the truth of it, Alfred wrote. *He wants to stay here. The thought of returning to his wife is torturing him. He was telling me about his troubled past with women. When he was younger his mother warned him against courting mill girls. Practically forbade it.*

Her husband Walter took her side, and as Danny had so much respect for his step-father it seemed he was obeying him as much as his mother. Whoever the lad had eyes for, his mother did not approve. When he finally left Gee Cross, he was almost forty, lonely, and yet a novice in matters of the heart. He told me all this. He fell for Flora and, he now admits, married her in haste. He was in too much of a rush, he said – he was desperate for a wife, and a family. She had him over a barrel. She spent his money, threatened to leave him, even assaulted him. She's a bully. Poor Danny wouldn't protect himself, he wouldn't lay a finger on a woman. Have you ever met Flora? It's far from a happy marriage.

I remember passing the letter on to Ada and watching her reaction. I could tell that, just like I had done, she was thinking of the occasions when we'd seen Danny with bruises on his face, and burn marks on his hand. And when twelve months earlier he had declined our invitation to bring his wife to Isabella Street for Christmas dinner.

By the February of 1918, the fourth year of a war that was supposed to last a matter of months, the port of Manchester was busier with troop ships than those carrying goods. American soldiers were landing regularly in Salford Docks whilst there was a dwindling supply of foodstuffs for the population. Just like everybody else, Ada and I were given a ration book which limited our access to sugar, meat, dairy products and, of all things, tea. The only consolation was that reports from Germany indicated that their people were having an even more difficult time of it. Russia's exit from the war had been offset by the arrival of the Americans, and we were told that everything in Germany, from manufacturing capacity to morale was in crisis. We began to believe that for all the fighting still to come, this year really would see the end of the war and an Allied victory.

Frustration in the form of the ration book was swept away when, with no warning, Alfred appeared at our door, grey of complexion and somewhat lopsided of posture, but grinning from ear to ear. Squealing like a child with a birthday surprise, Ada ran to greet him, smothering him with kisses and clinging to his neck. I waited my turn to embrace him, tears forming in my eyes. As I held him I could feel what I had suspected: his left arm was missing, his coat sleeve hanging limply at his side, a fatuous tube of worsted sewn neatly into a pocket.

"It could have been worse, Father," he said, pulling away and noticing my expression. "It could have been my right arm."

I could not stop myself looking down at my stump of a hand in its snug leather glove.

"Hell, it could have been my head," he was saying. "I could have been a dead man."

"Don't talk like that, Alfred," said Ada, dabbing her eyes with a handkerchief. "Come inside. I'll put the kettle on. Your father'll see to your bags. Let me help you off with that heavy coat, and have a good look at you. Whatever state you're in, my darling boy, thank the Lord you're here to stay."

Alfred was not for moping around the house for very long in spite of his mother's pampering – perhaps even because of it. His sleep was fitful, his moods uneven. He shaved off his moustache, only to let it grow back again. She did the best she could to feed him up, fetched him books to read and even bought him a new shirt or two. When the springtime came and he was inclined to take in the fresh air and walk further afield in the sunshine, his healthy complexion returned and he began to sleep more soundly.

Although the postal service to and from northern France, as we knew only too well, continued to be erratic and unreliable, he was determined to keep up a written correspondence with Danny Harrop. One day in March a certain letter arrived for him, which he brought down to the table at teatime, willing to share the contents with me:

Rouen, 5th March 1918

My dear Alfred,

I hope you are well and recovering from your bad time over here. As you say, at least the war is over for you, you did your bit and you can look forward to the next stage in your life.

I've been doing a lot of thinking about the next stage in my own. As you know, the hours drag by very slowly in this place and there's plenty of time to think. Too much time to think. Being with Marie-Anne is a blessing. It's the only thing that makes life worth living!

I've got a big decision to make, Alfred. After Easter they're transferring some of the nurses to the hospital in Le Havre, including Marie-Anne. Don't ask me why. She doesn't even know why. I don't know what I'll do without her. She's my strength. She's become my heart. We are desperately in love. We swore it!

I am on the mend. They've given me crutches and I'm learning to get along with them. I've started to sleep better and have an appetite again. They'll discharge me soon but I'm not going back to Blighty in an army truck. I'm a volunteer, I can resign if I want to. In any case I'm no use to the tank regiment no more. I've been told as much. I understand that, but I can still do a job as a mechanic somewhere. I can sit in a wheelchair and just about strip a tractor engine! Marie-Anne's grandparents have a farm in Normandy, not much more than seventy miles from here. She lost her father in the first months of the war and her mother is in an institution. We've talked about me helping her grandfather or finding a job in a garage somewhere. Oh, for this war to end!

But first I must decide about Flora. I'm a married man. I have obligations, I know. Responsibilities. Would it be cowardly to leave her? Would it be a sin even? I know nothing about divorce, do you? They say it's something only rich folk can do. I wonder what dear Walter would say. Sometimes I think I can hear him telling me to be loyal to my wife. Write to me with your thoughts, my friend. I respect your opinion even though, as you admitted once, you knew so little of life before you lived in the trenches.

They say that spring will be decisive in this war. A big German push is expected. Do or die. We'll see. I hope to be far from here, one way or another. A farm in Normandy or likely Manchester, after all? It's killing me, Alfred. Please write back as soon as you can. I need to hear a voice of sanity!

Take good care of yourself, my friend,

Your one-legged comrade,

Danny

2

After we had eaten I asked to see the letter again. Alfred did not mind. I took it to my study and followed the childish handwriting from start to finish. I felt terribly sorry for Danny. He was in such a fragile state and in such a bind. He was stuck in a loveless marriage and his only way out was fraught with guilt. He needed advice, and for all his good intentions I did not believe that my son was the best man to provide it.

The phrases in his letter that struck me the hardest were the ones about Walter Rowbotham. *I wonder what dear Walter would say. Sometimes I think I can hear him telling me to be loyal to my wife.* The fellow had never stopped worshipping his teacher, his mentor, latterly his beloved step-father. I knew Walter as well as anybody and he would never have wished to be held in such unquestioning regard. He was a most respectable and admirable man, of course, but Walter was no saint. It was time that Danny was given the full story.

The following afternoon, directly upon my return from work, I settled at my desk to compose a letter to Daniel Harrop. I lit a cigarette and stared for a moment at the crisp, blank page in front of me. In my mind I had been forming and re-forming the sentences all day long, aiming for a balance somewhere between kindness and severity. There was no reason to keep the fact of the letter secret from Alfred, or even from Ada, but I was resolved that the contents would remain confidential nonetheless. Alfred's knowledge of Walter was no more than superficial and it would remain so. There was categorically no reason to tell him more. It was all from a generation past.

Right before me Danny's face appeared on the paper like the image from a magic lantern. I saw his scruffy hair, turned the colour of dust, and the vulnerability in his eyes. I saw his thick, greying moustache, and as he opened his broad mouth to smile at me, I saw his broken tooth, chipped a life time ago on the edge of a weaving loom. He was in no rolling chair, nor did he lean on a crutch: he had two strong legs, muscled and firm, ready to chase hard after a football on some muddy pitch on the east side of Manchester. He stood up and offered me a hand to shake. *Hello, Charlie*, he said softly, with a sense of wonder in his voice. *This letter you're about to write. It's not to me, is it?*

17th March 1918

Dear Danny,

I hope your convalescence is going well.

This may come as a surprise to you but Alfred shared your recent letter with Ada and me and we are all concerned that you reach the right decision in your dilemma. I hope you don't mind that I am writing to you with some advice that, of course, you have every right to accept or reject as you wish.

I know how much Walter meant, and still means, to you. He was a father to you for most of your life. As you know, I had the same feelings of respect and admiration for him: for his good sense, his good manners, his loyalty and his quiet wisdom. I can imagine his spirit hovering over you each time you weigh up your moral conundrum. Am I wrong to think that you are consumed with a duty to live up to his example?

You might remember that I was Walter's best man when he married your mother. The pair of us met several times in the days leading up to the wedding and spoke more openly than we had ever done before. On one such evening we were drinking in the Cheshire Cheese. He was becoming nervous, a little insecure about marrying so late in his life, and, strange for him, was taking more alcohol than he was ever used to. Needless to say, his mind was relaxed and his tongue a deal looser.

He told me the story of a girl he knew when he was a young man: Josephine, a working girl who frequented the streets by the canal near London Road Station. Walter taught in several Unitarian day schools in Manchester before he came to Hyde, as I'm sure he told you. Josephine had once been a pupil of his, a poor girl but bright-spirited. When Walter discovered what had become of her, he took her under his wing. Those were his words to me. 'I took her under my wing.' He found her a job as a shopgirl and sometimes kept her company when she had to look after her sick mother. He even paid her to cook for him now and then. She strayed back into prostitution, however, and when he found out he lost his temper with her. Quite what happened, I do not know, but I gathered the relationship became what you might call fiery. And Walter confessed to me that he had slept with her at that time. On more than one occasion. He was unburdening a lifetime of guilt on me, but who was I to judge him?

One evening she came to his lodgings with a black eye and bruises on her neck, blaming Walter and threatening to tell the school authorities. Of course, he was mortified but he refused to be blackmailed. The following night he was awoken by banging on his door: it was Josephine's brother – also a pupil of his from the past but now a fully-grown bargee – who had come to rough him up and demand money. Walter had no choice but to pay him off. It was hard to believe that all this was true but I swear to you, Danny, it is exactly what I was told.

The story did not end there. Some years later the brother turned up in Gee Cross. Somehow he'd discovered Walter's address on Gerrard's Street. Josephine was dying, apparently, and he had come to demand money to pay for a decent burial. Again there was violence. Walter had to lie to your mother about how his face had become disfigured. You might even remember that time yourself, Danny. Of course, Walter was the victim in this story, but a man who did not know him might well conclude that he brought it upon himself and was weak in succumbing to physical temptation.

It gives me no pleasure to recount this tale. Indeed, I have kept it to myself, as I swore I would do, until now. I divulge this truth only to reveal to you that Walter was no saint, no paragon. He was a human like you and me, with faults and frailties and insecurities. We both loved him, Danny, but we mustn't worship him. The very thought would have made him shudder. No father would want that. Don't put the fellow on a pedestal, Danny, and don't assume you know what his words to you would be now.

As for me, I wish the best for you. My only advice is to follow your heart. Is there a reason why Ada and I were never allowed to meet your wife? Ask yourself which of these two women, Flora or Marie-Anne, could you least afford to live without. Put social conventions, such as they are, to one side and be brave.

I don't expect an answer to this letter, Danny, but I know that Alfred values your friendship and continued correspondence.

From one Hydonian to another,

Good luck and much love,

Charlie Knott

Epilogue
1919

When the German army finally surrendered – exhausted, demoralised, desperate for it all to be over – and when the November armistice was officially declared, there was such a feeling of exhilaration that celebrations both organised and impromptu were held in Manchester, as in the entire kingdom, to savour the joy of victory. Once the singing had ceased, once the anticipation of seeing sons and brothers and fathers returning to these shores had given way to impatience, the overwhelming sense was one of quiet relief. At least this is how I read the mood. Thank God that torment is all over. All that suffering for so little reward. Thank the Lord you're coming home. Never again.

Parliament had already set in motion a mechanism to reward the dogged soldiers with a stake in the country's future: they were to be allowed the vote. In the summer of 1918, as the inevitability of the Germans' defeat became ever clearer, a new Representation of the People Act came into law, extending the franchise to all males over the age of twenty-one, irrespective of class or income. At the time I could not help myself giving a thought to my Uncle James and those men known as Chartists, who had petitioned unsuccessfully for voting rights eighty years earlier.

Very quickly a general election was announced. The war was over – a new peacetime government was needed to set the country on a path to recovery, a return to prosperity. In December Mr Lloyd George was chosen to remain as Prime Minister even though Mr Bonar Law's Conservative Party gained the largest share of the vote. The Labour Party won fifty-seven seats, their highest total so far and surely a sign of things to come. In Ireland the votes went overwhelmingly to the republican party, Sinn Féin: seventy-three seats were gained but the new M.P.s refused to attend Parliament. A breakaway government has since been declared in Dublin and the situation over there, for the time being at least, remains unresolved and febrile.

The new act was generous to women (all property-owning females over thirty years of age were given the vote), but not generous enough in the opinion of women like Ada. She herself could vote, and her ailing mother likewise, but her work with the suffragists, suspended during the war, has resumed with vigour. She volunteers in the area of publicity, providing articles for journals and organising speakers to address women's groups in the city. She insists her work will only stop when women and men have equal representation.

Meanwhile she continues to contribute to the choir of St Hilda's. The choirmaster is rarely spared her irritation. Lately they have been practising a selection of Sir Hubert Parry's *Songs of Farewell*, new works which, so says Ada, were written to be sung unaccompanied. Mr Tetlow insists that his good friend from Fallowfield be free to embellish the vocal in his own way. Ada says he is "muddying the waters" with inappropriate organ patterns. Mrs Windybank, the lady at the post office on Stretford Road, left the choir practice in a huff last week, threatening never to sing for "that dreadful man" again. As for me, I'll not hear a bad word against Mr Tetlow. As I oftentimes say to Ada: "You do know, it's quite conceivable that your grievously disparaged choir master actually saved my life!"

*

Trade is gradually returning to the docks: oil and food-stuffs, mercifully, from old far-flung pre-war suppliers, and large amounts of bulk raw cotton. Many of the mills that closed during the war have reopened, but by no means all. The signs are that the height of textile production in what was once called "Cottonopolis" has passed. Industry generally is recovering at a snail's pace. There is already grumbling about unemployment rates amongst many of our returning soldiers who were promised jobs.

Phoenix (Port of Manchester) Shipping Agency Limited (formerly Booth & Byrne) has renewed a healthy number of contracts, principally with European shipping companies. The Scandinavian freighters continue to dock at Pomona but already it has become a place to spot Mediterranean faces once more, to see vessels and hear voices from France and Spain and Italy.

Not so long ago I recognised the *Duchesse d'Aquitaine* berthed in Number Two Dock, looking as gracious as an old maid on a *chaise longue*. She had not been seen in Manchester since the days before the war when I was once invited for an evening meal in the company of the mischievous captain, Jean-Jacques Puybonieux. She was no longer on our books but I could not resist a closer look. Smoke was rising in wisps from her funnel and on the wharf a few of her crew were milling about smoking French cigarettes, sheltering where they could from the drizzle, while dock workers were waiting for a crane to start a loading operation. I introduced myself to one of the crew: he was a scrawny fellow with little English but he understood that I was requesting to board. He waved me up the gangplank without a second thought and ambled back to join his shipmates. It appeared that a grey suit, a starched collar and a sober necktie was enough to create an impression of authority; perhaps he mistook me for police detective.

On board I found the captain, an earnest young officer with a clipped beard and piercing eyes who indulged my curiosity with great charm. A dark-skinned youth produced cups of very strong black coffee for us both as we chatted in the captain's quarters – a space that remained familiar to me. The circular table was still there, edged closer to the dining room wall, its chairs tucked away, sheltering under its solidity. Hanging in the very same spot, Eleanor of Aquitaine stared out from her portrait, the warmth of her smile, captured by a Flemish artist in the seventeenth century, still perfectly intact. Only the silver candelabra was missing.

It was explained that the ship had been laid up for most of the war years in Bordeaux. In the meantime, Puybonieux had taken up a commission with the French navy (in spite of his age), and he served on a cruiser which patrolled the Mediterranean. Successfully, I was told, until it was sunk in a naval battle in 1917. He was lost, very sadly, with the rest of the crew. I had only met the man once, but sitting on board the *Duchesse* in the very room where he had made gentle fun of my attempts to eat *spaghetti*, I was reminded of his humour and his kindness. I do believe that the young captain sensed my sadness.

Osmund Pollitt retired from the company last Christmas. I was sorry to see him go as he had been kind to me, especially in my early days at Booth & Byrne. He and his wife sold their house and went to live in Cleveleys: a place with a view of the sea, apparently, and just half a mile from their daughters' hotel. Mr Pollitt's replacement is rather younger than me. Ada encouraged me to apply for the post, and even though I did write a letter in that regard, I knew it lacked conviction and it came as no surprise when I was not invited to be interviewed. The job of managing director comes with a position on the board and I was aware that someone like me would not be welcome there. I have gone as far as I am allowed. The new fellow previously worked in one of the big banks on King Street. His family own a textile mill somewhere in North Manchester. He was educated at a university, of course, and he sounds like he was. They might have given the vote to all the Tommies back from the battlefields, but the English class system is still alive and well.

There is now a feeling of optimism with the plans for the resumption of professional sport. In spite of his move, Osmund Pollitt assured me he would be renewing his membership of Lancashire County Cricket Club. There was a decent railway link between Blackpool and Manchester Victoria, he confirmed, and he intended to watch several of their matches this summer. The Old Trafford ground was used as a Red Cross hospital during the war but I believe all vestiges of that facility have been removed and the place is being eagerly readied for the start of the new season. Similarly, it is expected that the Football League will restart in the autumn. For now the so-called non-competitive matches, arranged since 1915 to boost morale on the home front, go on. For the time being, Manchester United fulfil their fixtures in the Lancashire Section. Flyers are posted in the streets around the docks and all over Trafford Park advertising games. One such caught my eye only a few weeks ago: it was for a match against Liverpool F.C. Such is my emotional state these days, it takes very little to jog a memory, to evoke a sentimental reaction. And so it was that I was immediately transported back to the afternoon Mulloy and I had spent standing on the terraces at the football ground watching the home team take on the visitors from Merseyside. And inevitably my mind wandered to the second occasion: late April 1915 and the evening of that season's last hurrah. I saw once again the four of us, part of the crowd swarming to the ground: Mull, the Liverpudlian, Danny Harrop, whose passion for football far exceeded my own, for my presence was born out of curiosity as much as anything, and tagging along like an energetic puppy, my son Alfred. The four of us, laughing and joking and bantering about the last of the toffee brittle – four men now scattered and battered by the storms of our troubled times.

Alfred tells us he is fine – recovered, back on an even keel – but I know he suffers from nightmares and periods of depression. He has lost his job on the *Courier*; the newspaper ceased publication in 1916. However, he has submitted several articles on the subject of his experiences in France (brilliantly written, I must say) to *The Evening Chronicle*. They published one of them and the editor has invited him to assist one of their news reporters on a kind of six-month trial. Quite how he manages with one arm I do not know. He has ambitions to write for *The Manchester Guardian* one day. He heard the celebrated editor Mr Scott speak on the ethics of journalism at a public meeting at the Town Hall and came home altogether inspired.

Meanwhile he spends a good deal of his time at the theatre. It seems to be where he is happiest. There's a small flat above the Gaiety where he stays from time to time, especially if there is a production running, so several days can pass by without us seeing him. He is writing a play, collaborating with a friend who joined the navy during the war. It has absolutely nothing to do with warfare, however, being a kind of comedy, he says: a light-hearted murder mystery set on a transatlantic liner. There is a title but it escapes me for the moment. Something witty about double-crossing. When he is at home he likes to help his mother in the kitchen. Now he is learning how to bake cakes. With one arm! He's his mother's son and always will be. He joined her at one of her suffragist meetings quite recently, claiming it was for journalistic purposes. He must have been amused to see how the placid woman who fries his breakfast eggs each morning could transform herself into a titan of the sisterhood.

Alfred received a letter from Danny Harrop a week or so ago which he was happy to share with me. He is living in Normandy with Marie-Anne and her grandparents on a small farm near a town called Vimoutiers. He set himself up there before the war ended, before Marie-Anne could join him, working as a mechanic in the only garage left open in the town for lack of manpower. For the farmers and the older generation left behind he was a godsend, repairing their tractors, motor cars, bicycles and even long-abandoned sewing machines. In the letter he explained where Vimoutiers was. Alfred was encouraged to consult an atlas in the newspaper offices. It lies in the middle of rolling dairy pastureland about eighty miles south-west of the city of Rouen. Danny was eager to tell Alfred, cheese lover as he knew him to be, that the neighbouring commune was a tiny place called Camembert.

In the final paragraph I read Danny's best news. He was happy with his new family and would never come back to England. He was learning French, was popular with the local folk amongst whom there was no judgement as to his marital status. He and Marie-Anne lived, he wrote, "on a cloud of peace", unbothered by prejudicial remarks, loved by all their neighbours. And he was a part of a genuine family at that: *I'm a father! Can you believe it, Alfred? Marie-Anne gave birth a week ago to a sweet boy. Our little son, named Alain, after her dear, departed father.*

Ada and I wandered up to Hullard Park on Sunday last. It was a cold, bright day and the sky was as sparkling a clear blue as I have seen it. The birds were out, tweeting and twittering and having a ball in the shallow puddles. On one side of the park was a bank of daffodils, their golden yellow flowers already peeping out like shy little girls giggling behind a curtain. A workman was rolling a mower over the bowling green, tongue poking out between his lips in concentration: the first light cut of the season. I stopped and gave Ada a little kiss on the cheek, which surprised her.

"What's that for?" she smiled.

"Spring's in th'air," I replied, for indeed it was.

Meanwhile, there will be many events later in the year to commemorate the centenary of Peterloo, that sorry date in our history when a peaceful assembly, agitating for a working man's share in our country's so-called democracy, was brutally dispersed by sabre-wielding soldiers. They are events I am looking forward to. There's to be a procession to Platt Fields and a gathering of the Manchester & Salford Independent Labour Party at the Free Trade Hall. I hope to attend both if I am able. There will be a celebration of the achievements of the Chartists, although I am not sure that "celebration" is the right word. To celebrate something that is a birthright of every Englishman? It will be one hundred years since working folk marched in their multitudes to demand a vote in elections to our country's parliament, and it took ninety-nine years for it to be granted!

I think of all those years throughout the last century – wasted years – and of those far-sighted fellows who thought they were so close to success, who thought that the establishment would listen to them, would grudgingly accept the reason in their arguments, only to be thwarted time after time. And in this city, I think of those who congregated at St Peter's Field on that warm Monday in August: all long dead, of course, every man with his banner held high, every woman waving her flag. And I think of their children, too, all passed now, those bright-eyed infants, washed and tidied up for the day, brought along to listen to the speeches, to witness the parades, to hear the rousing music: boys and girls, overwhelmed by such a crowd, clinging to their mothers' skirts, their hearts filled with hope for brighter days and better lives.

Charles John Knott
Manchester
March 1919

AUTHOR'S NOTES

When I finished writing *Blessèd are the Meek*, my novel of the Hyde Chartists, I had absolutely no intention of making that story the first of a historical trilogy. As for some kind of sequel, the events of 15th October 1887 at Deepdale, Preston, had intrigued me ever since I stood on the terraces at Ewen Fields as a schoolboy, and the opportunity to write a novel about the early years of Hyde Football Club was too tempting. And so *Twenty-six Nil*, a second Hydonian story, was conceived.

I have to confess that I had so much fun writing about nineteenth century Hyde and its characters (some real, some imagined), that a third book was an indulgent pleasure. A trilogy implies that there is a definite sequence of events running from first to third but in that respect my series is much looser. Indeed, Hyde features only briefly in *Cheshire Cheese and Camembert*, the final novel. There are links among the characters, however: friendships and family relationships which bind especially the first story to the last. I was keen to tie up loose ends from the first two novels (and there are several) and take the narrative into the twentieth century. Charlie Knott, a child at the start of *Blessèd are the Meek*, is the middle-aged narrator now living in Manchester, telling a story that spans the years of the First World War. The father-son dynamic is a timeless theme running through the book. Meanwhile, the historical background is one in which modernity has arrived from the days of candlelight and horses to an age of motor cars and machine guns, telephones and tanks. And one in which the horizons of modern man have broadened with each decade, represented by growing international trade, the availability of 'exotic' foodstuffs and adventures in foreign fields – even if months spent on the front line in Belgium or northern France were far from a holiday. From parochial life to wider horizons. From Cheshire to Camembert.

As an amateur historian, I found researching the story to be illuminating and enjoyable. I learned a great deal about the early part of the twentieth century and was able to crystallise ideas that had previously been no more than nebulous. I must mention the value of the following texts: *The Manchester Ship Canal* by Chris Makepeace, *A Hundred Years of the Manchester Ship Canal* by Ted Gray, *Letters from the Trenches* by Bill Lamin, *The First World War* by Robin Prior and Trevor Wilson, *The Western Front* by David Ray and *Tanks and Trenches* by David Fletcher. Incidentally, to see such weaponry for real, The Tank Museum at Bovington Camp in Dorset, is well worth a visit. In addition, both of the following academic studies found online were very helpful: *Sea Transport and Supply 1914-1918* by Michael B Miller and *Old Trafford: The Evolution of a Victorian Suburb* by Amanda Kay. I would also like to acknowledge help received from staff at Manchester Central Library and the old maps available through the National Library of Scotland archive.

Music has often been a source of inspiration in my writing; a lyric may fit exactly what I am trying to express, a mood may reflect the atmosphere I am aiming to achieve. Rarely have two songs chimed with the narrative as perfectly as they did for me in the latter stages of the stories of Alfred Knott and Danny Harrop. 'Soldier Boy' and 'Be My Friend' were both written and recorded by Free in the early 1970s. I would recommend them (and their entire catalogue) to anyone who enjoys blues/rock, for that short-lived band were, in my opinion, Britain's finest exponents.

On a more personal note, thanks are due to Glenda Wray, over many years a much-valued contributor to the West Yorkshire choral scene, for her insight into church music of the time. As always, I am grateful for the help, encouragement and editorial advice offered by my wife Heather and my brother Warren. And Honeybee Books once again provided support and expertise in the novel's publication, for which many thanks.

Brent Shore
June 2023

ABOUT THE AUTHOR

Brent Shore grew up in Hyde, a small town on the eastern edges of Manchester.

He studied Modern Languages at the University of Nottingham, where he also trained as a teacher. Following a varied career which took him via North Yorkshire and Bermuda finally to Dorset, he now channels much of his energy into writing fiction, both contemporary and historical.

He has published seven novels:

Shillingstone Station

Bailing Out

An English Impressionist

Blessèd are the Meek

Inappropriate Behaviour

Twenty-six Nil

Cheshire Cheese and Camembert

Visit: www.brentshore.co.uk

Contact: stories@brentshore.co.uk

Blessèd are the Meek

Brent Shore

The Plug Riots of the 1840s: violent, significant steps on working people's long road towards justice and equality.

Based on historical truth, *Blessèd are the Meek* reflects on the life of a man who lived through these times: James Shore, a machine mender in the cotton mills of Hyde, seven miles to the east of Manchester. Politicised by poverty and injustice, he became a Chartist, a rioter and a convict but his story amounts to far more than that of a lengthy prison sentence. A son, a husband and a father, he was a man who sacrificed his freedom for the prize of equality, who glimpsed its light in the distance, but who was born too early to bask in its glow.

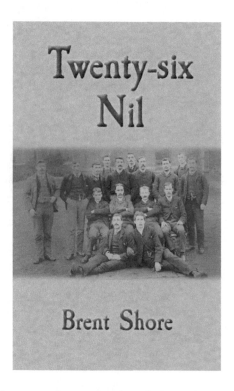

Twenty-six Nil

Brent Shore

1885. The young borough of Hyde has a brand new town hall and a fledgling football club. Within two years they have entered the prestigious FA Cup competition and face their first ever tie at Deepdale, the home of Preston North End, one of the most formidable teams in England.

But *Twenty-six Nil* is more than the retelling of the events of a remarkable football match. Offering a glimpse of life in a busy northern mill town, it is a tale of civic pride and companionship, and is a strangely heart-warming story of what was, after all, an almighty defeat.

MURDER!

SUSPENSE!

STEAM TRAINS!

"A great story line, with suspense and atmosphere right to the end."

"What a ride! I could not put it down until I had finished it."

MYSTERY AND MORAL DILEMMA IN 21st CENTURY WESSEX

"Excellent writing and characterisation"

"A very entertaining read; it gave me a great deal of food for thought."

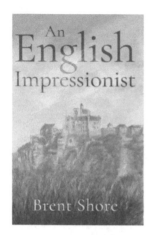

TO BE, OR TO SEEM TO BE?

"Penny is a wonderful character creation, a fascinating sociopath!"

"WOW! – what a brilliant read!"

HOW FAR CAN TRUST BE STRETCHED BEFORE IT SNAPS?

"A challenging subject, skilfully explored."

"I was hooked from page one; another excellent read."